1 MONTH OF
FREE
READING

at
www.ForgottenBooks.com

By purchasing this book you are eligible for one month membership to ForgottenBooks.com, giving you unlimited access to our entire collection of over 1,000,000 titles via our web site and mobile apps.

To claim your free month visit:

www.forgottenbooks.com/free112053

ISBN 978-0-483-71929-3
PIBN 10112053

LIFE'S MASQUERADE.

𝔄 𝔑𝔬𝔳𝔢𝔩.

IN THREE VOLUMES.

VOL. II.

LONDON:
CHARLES W. WOOD, 13, TAVISTOCK ST., STRAND.
1867.

LONDON:

BRADBURY, EVANS, AND CO., PRINTERS, WHITEFRIARS.

CONTENTS.

CONTENTS.

LIFE'S MASQUERADE.

BOOK II.—*continued.*

CHAPTER V.

M. GAUTIER.

THE door of the sitting-room was shut on the landing as Freddy passed, though through it he heard the strained voice of Mrs. Jerkins singing to herself. It was quite dark, and his heart began to thump away in his breast, with fear at the obscurity which his imagination peopled with many vague horrors. He bravely, however, made up his mind to go on; but remembering that two more black flights had to be passed before the very worst of all could be reached—the little dark hole where he was to sleep—his heart sunk within him, and he paused, uncertain how to act. Barbarous as was Mrs. Jerkins's voice, it sounded almost sweet amidst the darkness. Now and then he could hear the cry of Mr. Jerkins in the shop, reprimanding one of his sons; and even that dismal sound to the desolate lad wore an almost friendly tone.

Fearing, trembling, peering shrinkingly around him, Freddy stood for some three minutes irresolute, until at last, the one terror overmastering the other, he determined to ask Mrs. Jerkins, who still sang to herself, for a light. With this view he approached the door, of which he could discern the direction by the faintly-illuminated keyhole, and gave a trembling, stealthy knock. The singing ceased; there came a little pause, and then Mrs. Jerkins cried, " Who's there ? "

In the boy's heart, the fear awakened by the sound of that woman's voice, and the alarm consequent upon the darkness, divided their empire ; for a moment he thought to run away, but as he stood hesitating, Mrs. Jerkins again called out, " Who's that ? '

" It's me, ma'am."

" Who's me ? "

" Williams, ma'am."

The door was opened, and the big form of the woman stood before him. " You, hey? And what do you want ? "

" It's so dark I don't like to go up-stairs," was the trembling answer.

" Speak out; I can't hear."

Freddy repeated his observation, and added that he wanted a candle.

No sooner had this request been uttered than Mrs. Jerkins, putting her hand by her mouth, screamed out " Ge-orge!"

" Hallo!" answered a distant voice.

" Come here."

The door leading into the shop opened, and Mr. Jerkins came out. " What is it?" he asked.

" Here. Oh, come here!"

He obeyed, and then catching sight of the shrinking form of Freddy, cried, " Hullo! I thought you was in bed."

" Now," said Mrs. Jerkins, " you've heerd of himperance, haven't you?"

The husband looked from the boy to the wife, and back again, and then said, " Well?"

" Well, if himperance don't walk this airth in that boy's clothes, why," said Mrs. Jerkins, looking about her for a simile, and not finding one, she abruptly continued: " You've brought that young 'un here to ruin us—I know you have. Sich a thing wasn't never asked for afore by hany of your children, Mr. Jerkins, and if this is to be allowed——"

" But what is it?" interrupted the surprised Mr. Jerkins.

" Why this Williams has hactually asked me for a candle to go to bed with!"

" Oh! he has, has he? All right! Now young fellow, get you to bed at once. You'll ask for candles, will yer? You, who we're a feedin' and boardin' free of charge—candles, eh? Now, jist you get on to bed, and if ever I catch you at such extravagance again" — he shook his finger ominously at Freddy, and then crying, " Now, get on with yer!" pushed his wife and himself into the sitting-room, and shut the door.

Blinded with his tears, his little heart bursting with a thousand emotions, Freddy seized one of the banisters to guide himself by, and slowly commenced the ascent of the staircase. He had not advanced far, when he observed a light shining on the upper landing, and at the same moment a child's voice commenced singing to an accompaniment that seemed like the twanging of fiddle-strings.

Freddy paused and listened, then imagining to

take advantage of the light to illumine the way up, pushed forward, and stood upon the landing. Here he paused again, and stood still, looking at something which seemed to have awakened his curiosity.

The door, upon which was painted " Mons. Gautier," stood half open, and through the crevice Freddy could see a man seated on a stool, holding in his hand a guitar, the strings of which he occasionally swept with his fingers. On his knees lay a music-book, upon which a little girl who stood at his side was intently gazing. The man, whose shoulders were bent, wore on his head a velvet skull-cap, from which escaped a profusion of white hair. This gave him the appearance of age, an appearance, however, which was contradicted by his face, for looking at him thus, he seemed not more than forty-six or eight. He wore a long moustache, of which the colour being brown, gave him a singular and striking appearance. The child who stood near him was a perfect specimen of infantine beauty. Her hair, which, though now light, gave promise of being dark, hung in silken curls about her neck, which was exposed to the shoulders by the little white frock she wore. She was pale—too pale to

be satisfactory, though it injured not her beauty
—but the whiteness of her brow and cheeks only
seemed to set off the brilliance of her southern
eyes, and the ripe redness of her chiselled lips.
She was singing one of those simple French
songs, which end with " tra, la, la ! " and whenever she came to this chorus, she would look up
at the man with a smile, who would gravely nod
time, and then say, " *Bien, fort bien.*"

There was something so charming in the music
of the song, something so winning in the appearance of the singer, something so benevolent in
the aspect of the man, that Freddy's heart suddenly felt cheered within him. He `forgot his
terrors, and stood irresolutely at the door, the
confidence and the bashfulness of childhood
sometimes urging him to enter, sometimes dis-
suading him.   But whilst he stood thus debating,
the song ceased, and the man looking at the door,
said, " *Cherie, vas fermer la porte.*"   The girl
obeyed, but before closing it, peeped out, and
said, in French, " Oh, how dark it is ! "   " It is
always dark at night," replied the man.   But
even as he spoke the little girl had caught sight
of the boy, who stood half concealed in the shadow
of the doorway.

"Is that you, William?" she said, in English, but with a strong foreign accent. "Or is it James?"

"Who are you talking to!" asked the man.

She answered, in French, that there was one of the boys from downstairs on the landing. "*Comment!*" said the man, "what does he do there?" "Who are you?" asked the little girl, alarmed at Freddy's silence. He came out into the light, and the girl cried out, "Oh, papa, here is a strange boy in the house."

Papa came to the door, and seeing Freddy, asked him who he was.

"Frederick Williams, sir," answered Freddy.

"Do you belong to downstairs?"

"Yes, sir."

"But I have not seen you before."

"I only came this morning, sir."

"Come in," said the man; "this must be a mistake. Such as you can't belong down-stairs."

Freddy entered, and the man, closing the door, resumed his seat, bidding the boy to take the little chair opposite him. The girl came and leant upon her father's knee, staring at Freddy with all the might of her big eyes. Though the man was French, he spoke very excellent English.

"My name," said he, "is Gautier. This is my daughter Rosalie. What is your name?"

The boy had told him once, but he had forgotten it. "Frederick Williams."

"A very pretty name; are you going to be a linendraper?" Freddy, who was ignorant of the business, said he didn't know.

"Who is your papa?"

Here again was Freddy nonplused.

"And your mamma?"

Nor could he answer this.

"I belong to Miss Godstone," he said.

"This is a curious child," said M. Gautier, in French. "And what were you doing, my child, outside?"

Freddy said that he had been frightened to go to bed in the dark.

"And did they want to make you?"

"Yes, sir."

"Oh, *les barbares!*"

"*C'est un bel enfant,*" said Rosalie.

"Ay, there is some mystery about him, I'll swear. He neither knows his mother nor his father; and it is apparent that he is infinitely above the business below, and the *bête* that conducts it."

This was said in French, and then in English M. Gautier commenced again to question Freddy. Won by the benevolence of his inquiries, the boy slowly proceeded to open his heart, and before long had disclosed in his childish way all that he knew of himself, his present, his past.

"Are . you hungry, my child ?" asked M. Gautier.

"Yes," said Freddy.

M. Gautier whispered to his daughter, who ran to a cupboard and brought out a loaf and a pot of jam. Then he proceeded to cut three slices, which he spread with a thick layer from the contents of the jam, and giving one to each of the children, took the last himself.

At this moment there was heard the sound of footsteps on the stairs, and shortly after somebody knocked at the door. Freddy turned pale and trembled; he thought it might be Mr. Jerkins. M. Gautier noticed his alarm, but made no remark.

"It is William !" said Rosalie; "come in."

William, otherwise known to my reader as Bill, entered the room, his fat face lit up with a smile. On seeing Freddy, he stopped short, threw up his hands, and uttered an ejaculation of surprise.

" We've got company, you see," said M. Gautier, with a smile.

" I suppose you came in for a light? " said Bill.

" Yes," answered Freddy.

" Now ain't it hard," said Bill, appealing to everybody, " that father won't allow us no lights ? Jist as if we was cats, to see in the dark."

" I am afraid he's mean," observed M. Gautier.

" You may be sartin' of it," replied Bill.

" Here's your supper, Bill," said M. Gautier, cutting a slice from the loaf and putting some jam upon it. " And now I'll light you up if you're ready."

Bill took the bread, and having bowed, made towards the door.

" You needn't say anything to your father about this little child's visit to me," said M. Gautier.

" Mum's the word with me," answered Bill. " I'm ugly, but I'm honest."

With which assurance of his perfections and

his imperfections Bill went out of the room, followed by M. Gautier, who held a lighted candle. It was evident that Bill made these nocturnal visits first of all to be cheered inwardly and then to be illumined outwardly. This argued very well for the disposition of M. Gautier.

When the Frenchman returned to his apartment he found Rosalie standing before Freddy, who had just concluded a long yawn, and addressing him. What she said he did not hear; for she ceased on his entrance. He had heard, however, the yawn.

"You are tired, my child," he said; "where is your bedroom?"

"'Upstairs,'" said Freddy, drowsily.

"Come; Rosalie and I will see you safe; and tuck you up, too, eh, Rosalie?"

Rosalie answered with a sweet smile.

Then the father, taking Freddy by the hand, went upstairs with him, followed by Rosalie. When they entered the little hole, surnamed a bedroom, M. Gautier said, "Is this it?"

"Yes," said Freddy.

"*Pauvre petit!*" sighed the tender-hearted Frenchman. "Ah! there are no sheets to your bed." Then he seemed to reflect for a moment, and presently whispered to Rosalie, who ran downstairs. After a short absence she returned with a sheet.

"The blanket," said he, in French, "won't hurt me so much as it will him." Then taking the sheet which Rosalie had fetched from his bed he doubled it up, and placed it under the blankets. Then he undressed the little boy; who immediately got into his rude bed. "Don't you say your prayers before you go to sleep?" asked M. Gautier.

"I was never taught," answered Freddy.

"May I pray for him?" whispered Rosalie.

"Certainly, my darling," said the father.

Rosalie knelt down, and covering her face with her little hands, repeated with much devotion a short prayer.

Freddy watched her with his large eyes, and when she rose he said, "Was that for me?"

"Yes," answered Rosalie.

"Oh! how kind you are," and the little fellow's eyes were full of tears.

"Good-night," said M. Gautier.

"Good-night," said Rosalie.

They were about to leave, when Freddy looking

at Rosalie, said that he wanted to whisper to her. She bent her head down and he said, " May I kiss you ? "

She glanced at her father. " He wants to kiss me, papa. May he ? "

" Yes, my child."

The two little mouths met, and Rosalie's curls enveloped for a moment the smiling face of the boy.

A tear trembled at the corner of the honest Frenchman's eye, and he murmured to himself, " Of such is the Kingdom of Heaven." Then as he went downstairs he said to Rosalie, " I will have a talk with Mr. Jerkins to-morrow."

Though Freddy's dreams were that night haunted by a vision of Rosalie, he little dreamed of the influence she was destined to effect upon his after life.

CHAPTER VI.

LODGINGS TO LET.

M. GAUTIER, as the brass-plate on the street-door proclaimed, was a teacher of French, German, and drawing. He had been at Fernley eight months, though during that time he had succeeded in getting only two pupils. These were two middle-aged spinsters, who had read his advertisement in the "Fernley Chronicle," and who, imagining that all adventitious ornaments had a certain use in rendering less distant the prospect of matrimony, boldly plunged into the three accomplishments, paying the professor for the instruction of the same four pounds a month. Having, on his arrival at Fernley, seen "Lodgings to let" up at the house of Mr. Jerkins, and on inquiry finding the charge sufficiently moderate, he took them. But from that hour it was his constant regret that he had done so; for Mr. Jerkins, incited by his wife, was for ever threatening this poor man to raise his rent, swearing that the sum he was then charging was simply ruining him, and vowing that he must have been mad not to have known how better to value his accommodation. All this M. Gautier would listen to with a smile, then shrug his shoulders and say, " Very good; I will go somewhere else."

Then Mr. Jerkins's frown would relax : he would endeavour to look gay, and would remark, "Aha! no, don't leave us. I'm a poor man, with five young 'uns and a missis to feed and clothe, and I therefore likes to make as much as I can hout of everythink I touches. These are 'ard times, sir "—and then he would bring out his favourite apophthegm, " socks ain't meat, sir, nor collars corn ;" and so he would proceed in a lengthy discourse concerning his poverty, and the motive of his wishing to charge more for his lodgings.

For the first two or three times M. Gautier listened to this man with patience, but after awhile finding his supplication to be uniform and constant, he framed a reply as laconic as possible, which he would return with the same energy as that with which Mr. Jerkins would torment him. " Look, you say you are a poor man: I am sorry, and I can pity you, for I also am poor. But I cannot give you more for your rooms. If you are not content, I will go: at once, if you will."

This, uttered in a determined voice, always had the desired effect; Mr. Jerkins would depart, muttering to himself about his five young 'uns and his missis. But on the following week, when he took his seven and sixpence from the lodger, he would renew his demand.

Three weeks before the arrival of Freddy at Fernley, the two spinsters suddenly took it into their heads to discontinue their lessons. Two motives urged them to this step,—firstly, they objected to paying their money, and secondly, they found that after three months' moderate diligence, their lines were still as erring, their knowledge of French and German was still as limited as before the bi-weekly visits of M. Gautier.

Dispirited at his ill-success, the professor put another advertisement in the "Fernley Chronicle," subjoining a little list of his instructions at reduced charges. But up to the present moment nobody had responded to the notice.

"If," said he to Rosalie, "I do not get a pupil

before the end of this week, we will return to Paris."

Rosalie clapped her hands, and said,—

" Oh, how charming !"

The father surveyed her with a sad smile. To the child the future assumed the aspect of pleasure ; to the man, of famine.

It so occurred that the day following the events narrated in the last chapter was that on which M. Gautier's weekly rent fell due, and punctually at nine o'clock there came a rap on the door, and Mr. Jerkins entered. A dim suspicion had tortured this man's soul during the past week that his lodger would be unable to pay his rent, being led to form this conclusion by his wife having observed that M. Gautier no more went out on Tuesday and Friday to give his lessons. He entered, therefore, with a face paled by doubt ; and, having made his bow, stood looking with an inquiring eye on his tenant.

" Ah, it is you, Mr. Jerkins," exclaimed M. Gautier ; " I am anxious to have a little conversation with you. Pray be seated."

This was rather unusual. Before, M. Gautier always anticipated the arrival of his landlord by piling up the seven and sixpence on the table, where

Mr. Jerkins would see it and clutch, leaving in its place a receipt already prepared. Now, there were no signs of any money at all. The doubt in Mr. Jerkins's soul seemed about to be realised.

"Yes," said he, gloomily, "I will take a seat;" and he sat down.

"I find, Mr. Jerkins," began M. Gautier, "that you have a new boy in your shop. May I ask if you know anything about him?"

Mr. Jerkins eyed the Frenchman suspiciously, and said, "Why?"

"Because last night I met him on the landing, and being surprised at his youth, his beauty, and his charming little ways, I asked him who he was; but his answers were so unsatisfactory that I could learn nothing from him."

"Humph!" said Mr. Jerkins, thinking of his seven and sixpence, and wondering if this were some ruse on the part of his lodger to escape payment.

"And isn't he gentlemanly, papa?" said Rosalie.

"Yes, completely so. But do not think me impertinent in asking you these questions, Mr. Jerkins; only the boy has so very much interested me, that I feel quite a desire to know something

about him. In the first instance, you must confess that he is a great deal too good for your
trade."

"Yes, a dog's too good for it," growled Mr.
Jerkins, who was always pleased than otherwise
to hear his business decried. "But what's he to
you that you want to know all about him for?"

"Well, I'll tell you. I am interested in the
little fellow, and wanted to ask you to take pity
upon his tender years, and treat him kindly. He
has, at least so I gather from him, neither father
nor mother to protect him; and whoever has had
the charge of him must," said M. Gautier, red
with indignation, "be a monster of cruelty to
dismiss him into the world at so early an age."

"Well now," quoth Mr. Jerkins, "I likes to
hear all this too. May I jist ask wot business it
is of yours?"

"My compassion for his helplessness," said
M. Gautier, mildly, but not mildly enough to dis-
guise the profound abhorrence of the creature
who sat before him, that was expressed in his
voice—"must plead my excuses. Last night I
met this little creature shivering outside on the
landing, without a light, beset with the thousand
fears that attend children in the dark. I lighted

him up to the crevice that you have assigned him
as a bedroom, and there found a mattrass for his
bed, with a rug to cover him coarse enough to
scratch the skin from his limbs.   Now I thought
it was hard for a little fellow, perhaps far away
from his home—or worse, perhaps without a
home, to be treated like this.   And as he seemed
a good boy, I determined to ask you to be gentle
and kind to him, and act in the manner that a
kind and goodhearted man would act towards a
little defenceless, harmless infant."

Whilst he had been speaking two emotions had
been waging war together in Mr. Jerkins's breast
—rage at this meddling of a stranger in his private affairs, and fear that the money, of which he
could discern no signs, should not be forthcoming
at all.   Equally potent in their operations these
two emotions burst forth suddenly together, the
rage, however, being the stronger, making its
appearance first.

"Damme!" he cried, " but I should like to
know who you are, to come interfering in my
domestic matters ?   Hi'm a Henglishman born,
and this house is mine ; and damme, but no one
shall come troublin' me on matters that don't
concern anybody but myself; so I tell yer !   My

name is George Jerkins; I'm a linendraper and a honest man, and that youngster's my apprentice legal and square, and so I'll jist trouble you to leave him alone. And maybe, perhaps, now we're on the subject, you won't mind a lettin' me know when you're agoin' to pay me my week's rent, for which I came, and not to be troubled by the himperance of folks concernin' other peoples' matters."

He was fast running into incoherence, but fortunately saved his meaning by suddenly pausing.

M. Gautier eyed him with immense disdain, and putting his hand in his pocket, said,—

" You're an impertinent fellow, and I shall leave you to-day. Fortunately I gave you notice last week."

" Go when you like, and be d——!" shouted Mr. Jerkins, wild with rage.

M. Gautier approached him threateningly, and put his fist in his face,—

" Say that word again, and I'll screw that apology of a head off your shoulders!"

He looked so completely as if he would execute his threat, that Mr. Jerkins fled precipitately behind a chair, crying out:

" Give me my money—give me my money, and go !"

" Here are six shillings; I have no more ready money about me. I expect my remittance from Paris to-day; in the meanwhile take this."

"No, I won't take a sixpence less than my money you owe me. You've insulted me to rob me—I know yer !" and Mr. Jerkins glared infuriately at M. Gautier from the back of the chair.

M. Gautier shrugged his shoulders. "What time is it ?" he asked Rosalie, who had shrunk into a corner terrified at the appearance of Mr. Jerkins.

"*Dix heures moins un quart*," she answered, consulting a little watch which she drew with a trembling hand from her bosom.

" In a quarter of an hour the French post will be here. Go downstairs and in half an hour return, and you shall have your eighteen-pence; by that time we shall have packed up ready to go."

Mr. Jerkins glanced angrily about him; then considering that the course suggested to him was the best to be adopted, he turned upon his heel, and suddenly swung himself out of the room.

" Oh, what a bad man !" said Rosalie.

"Yes, darling; but let us now pack up. Please God, to-morrow we shall be in Paris."

"And the little boy, papa?"

"Ah! nothing can be done for him. We must pray for him, and leave him to his Father in heaven."

Rosalie said nothing, but had a little quiet cry to herself as she leant over a trunk, putting some things away in it. After a bit she put her hand in her pocket, and glancing around to see if her father were looking, pulled out an old purse, well worn at the sides, and opened it. In one of its partitions lay a little silver medal, such as they sell in France, with a figure of the Virgin on one side and some devout inscription on the other. Going to a drawer, she took out of it a thin slip of black silk, with which she threaded the medal, and then replaced it in her pocket. Her father meanwhile was engaged in arranging some books.

Half an hour later Mrs. Jerkins, her husband, and two sons, stood at the sitting-room window, looking out into the street.

"They're a comin' downstairs now," said Mrs. Jerkins.

"Send they break their necks afore they reach

the door," said Mr. Jerkins, devoutly. "Only think of his puttin' his fist in my face!"

"I hate them Frenchmen," said one of the boys. "Father, wasn't it Nelson as licked 'em at Waterloo?"

"Jim, you answer him; I ain't no scholard," said Mr. Jerkins.

"Oh, I knows as much as Jim!" said the boy.

"No you don't," answered Jim.

"That's right! quarrel!" said Mr. Jerkins.

"Who was it, then?" asked the boy.

"Foind out!" said Jim.

"That's what they call larnin', is it!" cried Mrs. Jerkins, slapping Jim's face.

"Here they are!" shouted Mr. Jerkins. And the four heads bobbed together at the window to look at the Frenchman and his daughter, who were walking towards the little hotel in Cork Street, followed by a sturdy man loaded with a trunk and a carpet-bag. Here they were going to take the coach to London.

But a little scene had occurred below, which, though concealed from the eyes of Mr. Jerkins, shall be made known to my reader.

As Rosalie and her father stepped out of the side-door, they saw Freddy occupied in rubbing hard at the brass plate along the front of the shop, upon which was inscribed Mr. Jerkins's name and calling. The sight of this reminded M. Gautier that he, too, had a brass plate, which, in the hurry of his departure, he had nigh forgotten. So, peeping into the shop, he perceived Bill behind the counter, to whom he beckoned. Bill came out.

" Have you such a thing as a screw-driver ? "

" Oh, yes."

" Will you procure it for me ? "

" Oh, yes." And Bill sped away. In a few moments he returned. " What is it for ? " he asked.

" To remove my plate from the door."

" Why ? "

" I am going."

" Going !" cried Bill.

" Yes."

" Oh, no, don't go."

" I am sorry to leave you, Bill," said the Frenchman, goodnaturedly ; " but unless you can secure a politer father, it would be impossible for me to remain here."

Bill seemed heartily sorry, and stood mopingly at the shop-door watching the operation of unscrewing the plate.

In the meanwhile Rosalie had been talking to Freddy. "We are going away," said she; "we are going far away across the sea."

"Shan't I see you again?" asked Freddy.

"Ah, who knows!"

Freddy burst into tears. "I am so sorry you are going; you are so kind, and I love you so."

"Rosalie!" said M. Gautier.

"Yes, papa!"

"Do not talk too much to the poor little fellow; it will only make him grieve more when we go."

"Only two words, papa!"

"Very well."

Rosalie approached the boy, and said, "Do not cry, little Freddy, we shall meet again. Look! here is a pretty present I give you. Put it round your neck—quick: so that nobody may see it. When you are by yourself, then you may look at it." She drew the medal from her pocket, and running the guard over his neck, slipped it into his hands. His large eyes gazed upon her, trembling with tears.

"May I keep it?" he asked.

"Oh, yes, until we meet again; then you

must give it me back; it was my *maman* who
gave it to me."

"Oh, I do love you so," said Freddy, "and
you are going away!" And again he burst into
tears.

"Rosalie, come away," said the father, who
had stood a silent spectator of this little scene—
though he had not observed his daughter's gift;
"we are ready. *Partons!*"

Once again she turned to Freddy. "Good-
bye," she said.

"My hands are dirty," he said; "let me kiss
you with my mouth."

These two children were almost of the same
height: the boy, perhaps, the least bit taller
than the girl. She approached him, and their
lips met.

"Good-bye," said she, crying.

"Good-bye," answered Freddy, with his eyes
also full of tears.

M. Gautier did not dare address the little
fellow. He nodded to him, and tried to smile;
but the attempt was stifled by the spectacle of
Mr. and Mrs. Jerkins's head at the window
above. So waving and kissing his hand to him,
these two—the young—the old—walked away,

leaving behind them a little heart aching with all the desolation of utter loneliness.

"Don't cry, little 'un," said a cheery voice by his side.

Freddy looked up, and perceived Bill's fat face smiling on him. "They're nice, dear people," continued Bill, "and I could cry, too, now they're gone. They've been kinder to me, little 'un, than they have to you, yet I don't cry. Now you jist be a man, like me; and when you've done the plate, I've a happle in my pocket we'll divide."

Freddy gulped down his tears, and went on polishing with his rubber. Before he did so, however, he turned his head, and looked down the street. The Frenchman and his daughter were just in the act of turning the corner. Before they disappeared, a handkerchief fluttered in the air.

"Who's that nasty little thing a waivin' to?" asked Mrs. Jerkins, with her cheek to the window, torturing her eyes to see down the street.

"To the apprentice, I suspect," answered her spouse.

"I'll apprentice him!" exclaimed the lady. "Did the Frenchman pay you your money?"

"Yes," grunted Mr. Jerkins.

"Well, now the rooms are vacant, I'll put up the card agin."

"I'll have no more furriners!" ejaculated Mr. Jerkins.

"No, stick to the Hinglish," exclaimed Jim.

"You mind your business!" retorted the father, angrily.

"Well, I warn't doing no harm."

"Yes you was. Leave the room, sir."

"It's that Frenchman as has put you out," said Mrs. Jerkins.

A probable conjecture. He had been at least a quiet tenant, and paid his rent regularly. "Hang him, and you, too!" quoth the husband.

"Thank yer," said his wife; "that's all the apprentice's doings!"

"I'll skin him, if he comes any o' his larks here!" said Mr. Jerkins, savagely.

"I wish to goodness the Frenchman had taken him with him," said the lady; "if he was so fond of him, why didn't he, hey?"

This is a question that may have occurred to my reader; one also that has occurred to me; though to it I am unable to give any reply. I can only conjecture that his means prohibited

this exercise of his benevolence; unless, perhaps, knowing the laws by which apprentices are
bound to their masters, and anticipating the
refusal of Mr. Jerkins to suffer the boy's departure, he cared not to solicit it—nor implicate
himself in a matter of which he could perceive
the trouble whilst ignorant of the result. At
least, this is all that I can offer in defence of
what may appear a conduct hardly benevolent.

CHAPTER VII.

THE RUN-AWAY.

THE blow that had befallen Freddy in the sudden departure of his so newly made friends, he did not sufficiently appreciate until the approach of the evening. The darkening rooms renewed all his terrors of the preceding night—terrors rendered more acute now that he remembered he should find no gentle voice, no cheery light to escort him to his little black den. When the evening meal had been despatched, the shop closed, and he ordered to bed, he mounted the stairs as usual, and gained the landing opposite the door of the Jerkins's sitting-room; but when he looked up into the blackness beyond, his little heart suddenly failed him, his knees smote together, and he sunk upon the stair, weeping piteously, though silently.

He had not remained long thus before the door downstairs was opened, and he heard the tramp of Mr. Jerkins and his sons ascending. They

came up tumultuously, for they were in the dark,
feeling their way up, sometimes stumbling against
a stair and sometimes knocking against each
other.   Having gained the landing, they opened
the door of the sitting room and passed in, unconscious of the presence of the boy, who had
cowered on their approach, and shrunk terrified
against the wall, stooping and holding his breath
and tears to avoid detection.

No sooner had the family assembled together,
than there commenced a hubbub of voices, the
result of everybody speaking at once, conspicuous
above which rose the upbraiding tones of Mrs.
Jerkins attacking her spouse.   Sometimes Freddy
would catch the meaning of the speaker, be it
whom it might, when a lull would come, and only
two voices speak at once; thrice he heard the
name of Gautier uttered, once by Mr. Jerkins,
who, by the dull sound that followed the remark,
seemed to have struck the table as he repeated it,
and twice by Mrs. Jerkins, both times in a shrill
voice, truly expressive of enraged contempt.
Then rose a hubbub, which lasted for several
minutes.   At last the door opened, and Bill came
out.   He paused on the landing a moment, and
put his ear to the keyhole of the door which he

had shut. Mr. Jerkins was saying something in an undertone. When he had finished, Bill suddenly re-opened the door, and popping his head into the room, cried, " I heard: all right. But hang me, if you shall hurt him; you may bully him as much as you like with your tongue, but blow me, there shall be no strikin' of him with fists whilst I'm here." Having said which, he pulled the door to, and passed up-stairs, almost touching Freddy without perceiving him.

The boy rose to follow him. Here at least was a companion; for Bill's room was in the garret, and next door to Freddy's. But he trembled, and again stopped. He knew little of Bill, more than that he had smiled on him once or twice, and had spoken to him in a manner that seemed kind after the voice of Mr. and Mrs. Jerkins. But though he perhaps guessed him to be no enemy, he was by no means sure of him as a friend; and moreover, the intense darkness of the little hole up-stairs, pregnant with the horrors that only Night can breed, and which only the imagination of little boys can perceive, came before him; slightly raising the hair on his head, covering his trembling body with a thin coating of perspiration, and glueing him to the spot where he stood, fearful alike to ascend or to remain.

Though Bill had pulled the door to, the latch had not caught, and it therefore stood the least bit ajar. From this interstice there shone against the wall, near the boy, a welcome strip of light, so welcome, that had it been tangible, Freddy could have thrown his arms about it, and clung to it as a friend at whose approach the evanescent, ghostly lights—nebulæ of the imagination which every eye can see in every darkness—disappeared together, with the terrors they provoked.

By the door remaining thus unshut, the voices of the inmates of the room were rendered more audible; and it was apparent that since Bill's departure, there were symptoms of the conversation being carried on more consecutively; Bill evidently having been the inciter of this social tumult, being the one voice in favour of that of which the other six voices were the opposers.

" So he's comin' the spy, hey ? " Freddy heard Mr. Jerkins's voice say; "a listenin' at the key-hole to his parient's conversation ? all right ! "

" I'd break his neck for sich a trick if I had the managin' of him," answered the voice of Mrs.

Jerkins. " But you've only got yourself to thank for this, Mr. Jerkins; he never did it afore——"

" Afore what ? "

" Afore you took in your young apprentice. Drat him ! look what he's brought us to ! "

" It's werry hard, father," said a chorus of two young voices, " that you should go aboardin' and feedin' this young 'un, when we ain't got nor a much to eat ourselves."

" Shut you up, cheek," cried Mr. Jerkins; " wot business is it of yours ? "

" That's how you're a treatin' your own flesh and blood," exclaimed Mrs. Jerkins, " whilst towards that young Williams you're all mildness and soft soap."

This must have been said ironically. But Mr. Jerkins had a mind unsusceptible of satire. " What do you mean ? " he cried.

" Why," answered Mrs. Jerkins, rather evasively, " I should jist like to put the question to anybody acapable of judgin' it properly, and ask him what treatment a youngster ought to get who did what this Frederick Williams has done ! "

" That's right, mother," said one of the sons, " stand up for us ! "

" So I will," answered the mother, in a voice

which, by its thickness, might have been taken to represent or express affection. "If your own father ain't proud of you, I am! and wot's more, I ain't ashamed to say so, neither, though it least-ways becomes me to speak out. And I ain't agoin' to mildly stand by and see you cut out of your father's affections by a young striplin' who only comes into the family to cause rows. Malice! I never seed such malice! Here, he ain't been with us twenty-four hours before our lodgers get discontented and go—mind you, after stayin' with us months, all the while satisfied, until *he* came."

Here Mr. Jerkins gave an angry growl.

" Then the next thing is his askin' for candles —a purpose to torment us—and p'raps to ruin us. Then he works upon Bill to set to and anger his parients,—hopposin' all we say, langhin' boldly in our faces—and then, to crown all, goin' out and clapping his ear to the keyhole to secretly listen to the private and confidential talk of them as bore and clothed him. And wot aggravates me is, that the lad was always steady and good before that young mischief came to eat our food and set us one against each other."

Here another hearty growl alarmingly testified

to the state of Mr. Jerkins's temper, and the pro-
gress made by the eloquence of his spouse, who
was now conversing tearfully.

" But I'd forget everything," she continued:
" I'd treat all that has taken place with contempt,
and forgive everybody, ay, wirtuously forgive
them. But when I remember that the head of
this family, the father of them boys, the proprietor of this business, the husband of me, has
had a fist shaken in his face, his nose threatened
to be pulled, his body perhaps kicked," said Mrs.
Jerkins, a want of actual facts leaving her imagination to supply her eloquence with visionary
probabilities, " and all this too by a Frenchman,
I say," said Mrs. Jerkins, turning her head away,
and addressing a corner of the room, " that it is
time something was done, and this matter stopped,
unless we wants to be snubbed by everybody, and
go to the bad as if we never belonged to the
good."

This peroration was evidently matured, and
matured with an acuteness of comprehension
that was made speedily manifest by its effects upon
the mind of the chief listener.

Bringing his fist heavily upon the table, Mr.
Jerkins exclaimed, with an oath, " Ay, it's just

as you say, and I was a blind fool not to see it afore. This young varmint has been the cause of it all—of course he has. The whole matter is as clear as daylight. He's been tellin' tales to the Frenchman, which has driven him away, and it's just as likely he'll go round to the neighbours, telling them lies about me, and, in course, ruining my business."

"The little wretch! That's him all over!" exclaimed Mrs. Jerkins.

"But I'll stop him," cried Mr. Jerkins, hoarsely. "I'll give him such a hidin' to-morrow as'll make him remember me the longest day he lives! The young bastard! I'll teach him to tell tales! Of course, he'll ruin us—don't I see it? But I'll lick him; he's got no friends but me, and I'll show him wot my friendship is!"

Here somebody laughed, and then there came a short silence. It would be by no means easy to describe Freddy's feelings as he heard this conversation. He was far too young to compre-hend the malignancy of Mrs. Jerkins's remarks, prompted by the influence of an ignoble jealousy, a villanous anger, a vulgar hatred, acting upon a base, coarse, and brutal mind. One fact alone remained horribly palpable to him, that to-mor-

row he was to be beaten, and beaten by a man
whom his childish instinct told him would inflict
the punishment with all the barbarity that cow-
ardly rage discovers towards inoffensive helplessness. This was the appalling terror that was to
crown the awakening of the morrow ; and as the
idea flashed across the boy's mind, a horrible fear
took possession of him; already he seemed to
feel the iron clutch of Mr. Jerkins on his arm ; to
see the uplifted stick, the brutal fury expressed
in the tradesman's eyes; conscious, above all,
that there was no hope of pity, no chance of
succour !

This was the ruling fear, all else was forgotten. Quick as thought he ran noiselessly
down-stairs, and lifted the latch of the side door.
It was not locked, Mr. Jerkins postponing this
duty until the last thing at night. The door
grated a little on its hinges, but the boy paused
not. Without looking behind him, without stopping to pull the door to, or leave it on the jar to
avoid the chance of his absence being discovered
by the noise, he gained the street, and with eyes
dilated by the maddening fear that possessed him,
without a cap on his head, and his hands outstretched before him, he flew down the road,

took the first turning that presented itself, and in an instant was lost in the darkness of the night.

At the same moment that he had disappeared from the street, a sudden current of air caused the door from which he had issued to close with violence, its noise in doing so being increased by a loose knocker that adorned its front.

" Who's there ? " shouted Mr. Jerkins, coming out on the landing, leaning over the banisters, and peering from under the candle which he held over his head.

Of course, there was no reply.

" Who's there ? " shouted he again.

" What is it, father ?" asked his four sons, popping their heads out of the door and looking at him.

" Jim," said Mr. Jerkins, " go down and see who's at the door." Jim demurred a little, but his father, with a frown, having repeated the order, he went edgewise down, the better, perhaps, to turn and flee should there be any cause for alarm.

" There ain't nobody here ! " cried he, when he had reached the bottom.

" Open the door and look out," cried the father.

Jim tremblingly obeyed, and after a rapidly nervous glance up and down the street, said, " No, there's nothing here."

" Well, that's odd too," exclaimed Mr. Jerkins.

" What is it ? " said his lady, looking out at the door.

" Didn't you hear that door bang ? "

" Yes," said the lady.

" Well, wot was the cause ? "

" Heaven knows," said the lady; " perhaps the wind."

" To be sure," exclaimed Mr. Jerkins, " it must have been. Now, somebody must have left that door open. Who was it ? "

" It warn't me ! " said a chorus.

" Who came in last ? " asked Mr. Jerkins. " Was it you, Dick ? "

" No, father," said Dick.

" Was it you, Paul ? "

" No, father," said Paul.

" Then it was you, Jim."

" I'll take my oath it warn't," said Jim.

" Oh, I know who it was," cried Dick.

" Who ? " said Mr. Jerkins.

" Why, the apprentice," answered Dick; " he was last in, cos he couldn't get 'is shutter-bolt to."

" I'll apprentice him! " cried the father.

" If I was you, I'd bring him down and make him shut it now, as a lesson for the future," said Mrs. Jerkins. " Wot right has he to go a makin' them noises at the dead o' night to disturb us ? "

" Oh, yes, bring him down, father," said the chorus.

" That's a good thought," said the father. " Jim, go you and fetch him ; here, take this light."

Jim, delighted with his mission, flew up-stairs; but after an absence of a few moments he was heard coming down again, and presently he appeared, descending at the rate of three steps at a time. " Oh, father ! " shouted he.

" Wot is it ? "

" The apprentice ain't in his bed."

" Ain't in his bed ! " screamed Mr. and Mrs. Jerkins together.

" No ! he ain't even been to bed, for the clothes isn't touched."

" Give me the light," said Mr. Jerkins, and away he journeyed up-stairs.

It is hardly necessary to say that he found

Jim's communication strictly correct. He went into Bill's room, and found him fast asleep. Having awakened him, he asked where Williams was. Bill drowsily answered that he did not know.

" Are you sure ? " asked the father.

" Why, what do you mean ? " asked Bill.

` " The apprentice isn't nowhere to be found; he ain't been to bed ; and that's what I mean," said Mr. Jerkins.

" Then he's bolted ! " said Bill.

" Bolted !   Why he's my apprentice ! "

" I don't care for that.   If he ain't nowhere to be found, he's gone."

" I'll break his neck, if I catch him."

" No, you won't."

" Won't I, though ? "

" For you'll never catch him."

" Why, you imperant devil, wot do you mean ? "

" I mean this," cried Bill, getting out of bed, and approaching his father in a menacing manner, " you're a bully and a coward; though you're my father, I tell you so to your face.   Only a bully would have threatened the poor little fellow like you did, and you're a coward for doing so.   You may frown—I ain't frightened of you. I tell yer, you're a bully, and I'm ashamed o' you. If you wasn't my father, I'd turn to and hide yer in a manner that should make yer remember for the future to treat little boys who can't defend themselves, well. You, a man!—bah! I'm ashamed o' you! Don't frown—I ain't .frightened, so I tell yer."

Bill was fourteen, his father forty. They were both of a height, but Bill was far the stouter and the broader. The father eyed him awhile in silence, and then said, " You leave my house to-morrow."

" I was a going without your permission. I've got a engagement as 'll bring me more money and better treatment than I gets here."

" You're a willin !"

" I ain't a willin !—no names, or I'll turn you out o' this room."

" You willin !" shrieked Mr. Jerkins, literally foaming with rage. "You scoundrel! *you* turn me out! *me*, out of my own house! Take that !" and he flung the candlestick with all his might at his son's head. Had it struck him it would instantly have killed him : but, fortunately for Bill, his father's aim was marred by his rage, and the candlestick flew wide of the mark, striking the wall and flattening its side by the collision. At the same time the father rushed at the son, and closing with him they both fell heavily to the floor.

It was pitch dark. The floor of the room shook with the struggles of these two unnatural combatants. Not a word was spoken. At last a voice cried out, "Let me go ! let me go ! you're stifling me—off with your hand—your hand !" At the same moment the room shook as with the movement of a form being dragged along the floor. There came a shock as of somebody pushed down. The door was closed, and then might be heard the sound of some one groping about. Suddenly a match was struck ; it flashed along the floor ; a hand grasped the battered candlestick, and ignited the fragment of candle it contained.

The glare illumined the features of Bill. He presented a ghastly spectacle. Blood was oozing from his eyes, nose and cheeks—the latter being lacerated and terribly torn as if by nails and teeth. He was examining his first finger, which dropped down from his right hand—plainly showing that it was broken. Taking a can of water which stood by the side of the bed, he emptied it into a bucket, and commenced bathing his face. The smart of the wounds by contact with the cold water must have been agonising, for he cried aloud, and hot tears fell from his eyes. There was blood upon the floor, and blood upon the front of his shirt which had been torn half off his back, and which was now connected only by the shoulder.

When he had concluded his ablutions, he took the candle, and looked out on to the landing. Nobody was there, and this seemed to please him, for he said to himself half-aloud, " Thank God, I ain't killed him ! "

This exclamation referred to his father, whom, after the struggle, he had seized by the collar, and thrust out of the room. Half-dead from the strangulation that must have ensued, had his son kept his grasp upon his throat a few moments longer, Mr. Jerkins suddenly found himself precipitated on to the landing, where he lay for a short while panting in almost the last stage of exhaustion. But thin, wiry men, such as Mr. Jerkins, are not long in recovering their breath, and it therefore followed that before many minutes had elapsed he was breathing pretty freely, though aching from his roll on the floor.

The truth was, Bill's injuries were infinitely more serious than his father's. The lad, unwilling to hurt his parent, yet being unavoidably compelled to act on the offensive, in order to defend himself, had striven rather to subdue his father than to injure him; whereas Mr. Jerkins, with the vindictiveness belonging to age, with the malignity belonging to brutal anger, and with all the ferocious passions belonging particularly to his disposition, had been far less careful of his son's welfare, biting, scratching, kicking him with a vehemence that the wounds on Bill's features, and the blue marks on his person, rather more than sufficiently demonstrated.

Mr. Jerkins, therefore, finding no bones obtruding about his form, gathered himself together, and with many a sigh, many a hearty malediction, many a heavy groan, he limped slowly down-stairs, and entered the sitting-room, where sat his wife and four sons wearied with waiting for him and the apprentice from whose presence they had reckoned upon extracting some considerable degree of amusement.

It would be worse than vain my hoping to convey to the reader in words the amazement, the consternation that seized these five persons at the grotesque spectacle presented to them in the aspect of the father and the husband, Mr. Jerkins. No language can describe it ; nor yet the frothy and furious manner in which he gave forth his narration of what had taken place ; nor the fury of Mrs. Jerkins who sat listening to him ; nor yet the disappointment, rage, and maledictions with which this worthy family contemplated and greeted the fact that the young apprentice had actually run away: thus depriving them all of the sport they had anticipated, first of all in seeing him tremblingly descend to close the door ; and secondly, in the sound thrashing that he was to have received the following morning.

"I'll have him hanged," said Mr. Jerkins, thinking of his son.

"We've got the fifty pounds, however," said his wife, with her thoughts fixed on Freddy.

"The scoundrel—the wretch ! to attack his father."

"He must have left his box behind him—and his things 'll do for you, Paul."

" Oh, my head, my head ! " groaned Mr. Jerkins.

" You had better go to bed, my dear."

And here let me drop the curtain. Not a dozen chapters could contain the whole of the dialogue that occurred after this last recommendation from Mrs. Jerkins. What the linen-draper swore to do was terrible indeed to hear. His threats of vengeance, firstly, on Bill for fighting him, and secondly, on Freddy for leaving him, were sanguinary and awful. He vowed he would not sleep in the house whilst his son was in it. But as there seemed no chance of his son leaving at any rate before daylight, and as nobody volunteered to accelerate his departure, Mr. Jerkins was at last fain to content himself by repeating his threats; and by swearing that he would have the county, nay, the whole country scoured for the runaway apprentice, if only for the satisfaction of half murdering him when he should find him.

But my reader will easily guess that all this was merely rage venting itself in empty talk; for to say nothing of the expense incidental to such a proceeding—an insurmountable obstruction had there been even no further impediment—

Mrs. Jerkins would certainly never have permitted her husband to do anything so foolish, being by no means desirous of having the apprentice back, unless for an hour, that he might just receive the castigation that this honest couple thirsted to bestow.

As for Bill, he was gone before they were up the next morning, and it may gratify my reader to know that from that day they never saw anything more of him.

CHAPTER VIII.

THE RUN-AWAY—*continued.*

THE course of this narrative returns to Freddy.

In small country towns such as Fernley, not many people are abroad much after half-past eight in the evening; for the shops close early; the streets, as a rule, are badly lighted; and hence one of the chief provocatives to retain people out of doors is wanting : for in this, it must be confessed, men and women resemble fish, who are easily collected together by means of a light. At all events, on this particular night, made memorable in our history by its being devoted to the flight of Freddy,—the one street in Fernley, with its few and minute ramifications, was almost deserted. Not even was a watchman visible; the only persons to be seen being perhaps an aged woman and a child, or a distant man, either ahead or behind, and just about turning some corner.

The distance from Mr. Jerkins's house to the uttermost limits of the town—that is to say, in the direction pursued by Freddy—was a walk of some six or seven minutes. At the rate at which our little boy was running, it was accessible in less than a third of that time; and therefore, ten minutes after Freddy's first start he was speeding along the London Road with the town to his left a large quarter of a mile away.

The night was quiet and fine. A warm southerly wind tempered to mildness the atmosphere, and in the east came slowly creeping up the silver moon, tinging the edges of the leaves with white, and rendering snow-like the road upon which the little runaway was travelling. Slowly he was putting out, one by one, behind the corner of the bend of the road he was taking, the lights of Fernley; and though to his left he could see amidst the obscurity rendered hazy by the moonbeams, the twinkling glare of an occasional farm-house window, to his right there loomed a heavy bank, which, topped by rows of tall trees, wore a very solemn and mysterious aspect.

When a child is under the influence of a powerful terror, the predominating emotion will dispossess its heart of those fears which under circumstances of a less exciting nature a present concurrence of events might have provoked. Though silence, darkness, and a strange country, were around him, the affrighted boy saw, felt them not, in the recollection of Mr. Jerkins and his threat. If his eyes were dilated with terror, —if ever and anon he glanced fearfully around him, it was not his present situation that alarmed him;—it was fear of the past, aggravated by an imagination which was constantly picturing the form of the ruthless tradesman behind, with outstretched hand ready to grasp him and immolate.

But fear is an exhausting emotion; and, when united to flight, it needs something more enduring than the frame of a child to sustain it long.

Freddy was now rapidly growing fatigued; he had been running at his fullest speed for at least a quarter of an hour; and at last, breathless and panting with weariness and alarm, he threw himself down against the bank, which had gradually declined to a few feet above the level of the road, his face bedewed with perspiration, and his little body trembling with excitement. He strained his eyes down the road he had just traversed, imagining every moment to see the form of the small tradesman running in pursuit of him; but there were no signs of anything at all resembling Mr. Jerkins, and a feeling of relief—of actual safety, took possession of the little fellow's heart. The night was very still: now and then, perhaps, the tall trees at his back, fenced in by a hedge running the length of the bank on which he was reclining, would sigh when a faint air whispered through their leaves ; or, far away, he would hear the occasional clear note of the bull-frog croaking its pæans to the cloudless skies.

The boy seemed to find his security in the moon. With face upturned, he watched with fixed eyes the brilliant and friendly orb, and sometimes fancied that the man in it, with his eyes, nose, and mouth, so clearly pourtrayed, looked down with a quaint and friendly smile, as if he knew him. But not for long; for gradually the face grew misty—the eyes went out, the nose disappeared, the sharp outline of the moon grew indistinct, and melted away into the skies that had become suddenly dark;—and it, and Mr.

Jerkins and his terror, became obliterated from the boy's mind, in the profound slumber that had seized and suspended all consciousness.

He had been asleep a quarter of an hour, when the sounds of footsteps and of voices speaking in subdued tones grew audible, coming along the road in the direction of Fernley; and in a few moments the moon revealed the figures of two men leisurely walking side by side. Each one carried a gun upon his shoulder, and over each back was suspended an empty sack. They also wore belts round the waists, from which gleamed the polished steel butt of a pistol; and their heads were enveloped in fur caps with lappets that hung loosely over their ears. A picturesque couple they truly were! Nor was their appearance rendered less romantic by the shaggy beards and moustachios that concealed the lower part of their faces. A little spotted spaniel walked gravely between them.

As they approached opposite to where Freddy lay sleeping, the spaniel uttered a short yelp and sprang forward in the direction of the boy. The men's eyes followed the movements of the dog, and in an instant lighted upon the form by the wayside.

One of them gave a start, and grasped his comrade by the arm.

"Jem!" he exclaimed in a whisper, "wot's that?"

"It looks like a ghost!" said Jem.

And in truth it did, though a ghost that it had never entered into the heart of man before to conceive. The boy was reclining precisely in the position in which he had fallen asleep. His curly hair lay floating upon his forehead, shading the closed eyelids whose long lashes lent an ineffable beauty to the marble pallor of the sleeping face. His lips were divided by his breathing, and their sad expression in one so young only rendered the whole countenance more beautiful. The little white hands were folded upon his breast, and one leg was negligently crossed over the other. Perfect as this picture was, its human loveliness was rendered divine by the silvery tint of the moon that seemed to envelope the sleeping child in a phantasmal veil of light.

The spaniel was sniffing at the boy's feet, but a slight whistle from one of the men brought it to his side.

"This is a queer go!" exclaimed the man

called by his associate Jem; "I wonder wot and who he is!"

"May be he's fallen out of one of them stars," said his companion, pointing up with his thumb and speaking seriously.

But this rudely poetical speech was received with a smile by Jem, who was evidently not of a poetical temperament.

"I tell ye wot," said he, "this youngster 'll be of use to us. He can keep watch, eh?"

"A werry good thought!" exclaimed his friend.

"Wake him up."

Jem touched the sleeper upon the shoulder, who opened his eyes,—and, seeing the weird, strange figures before him, leapt to his feet with a cry of alarm.

"Oh, where am I?" he asked.

"In werry good company," answered Jem. "Wot's your name, my covey?"

"Frederick Williams," answered the boy, rubbing his eyes and staring about him in bewilderment.

"Where do you come from?"

Freddy glanced at him with a terrified gaze. For a moment the dreadful thought occurred to him that these men had been sent by Mr. Jerkins in pursuit of him. In an instant he was upon his knees, praying them not to take him back to Fernley.

" Oh, you come from Fernley," said Jem ; " all right—get up, we ain't going there, so you needn't be afeard."

Then, aside to his companion, he whispered, " Some runaway schoolboy, I'll warrant. There'll sure to be a reward—we'll jist keep our eyes upon him, eh ? "

The other nodded back his satisfaction at the conjecture ; and then Jem, turning to Freddy, said,—

" It won't do for you to go a-sleepin' here— you'll catch the rheumatics in no time. So come along with us ; we jist want to give yer a little employment, and after that you shall have a supper and a good bed."

This was said in a gruff but not unkind voice. Freddy began to feel a little less alarmed, though he was still in a great fright.

" Can you blow ? " asked Jem.

Freddy glanced up with a puzzled face.

" Look here ! " continued Jem, putting his hand in his pocket, and producing a battered metal whistle ; "put this to your mouth, and blow—not 'ard—but blow."

Freddy did so, and produced a distinct and penetrating sound. There was something grati-fying in this to the child—and he looked up into the man's face and smiled.

"Brayvo !" said the man, heartily, tapping him lightly on the back ; " he's a regular brick—ain't he, Joe ? "

" Ay, that he is," answered Joe.

" How long have you been a lyin' out here ? " asked Jem.

" I don't know," said Freddy.

" Quite long enough," said Joe, " to get damp-like about the bones, eh Jem ? "

" Ay," said Jem ; " and he's such a fine young feller, that he shall have a drop of this, jist to keep the damp out." And saying this, he put his hand into a back pocket, and produced a flask. Then unscrewing the top, he poured a very little of the contents into the cup, and told Freddy to drink. " Don't sip," said he, " but swaller it right away down."

Freddy did so ; and the result was a great deal of coughing, a profusion of tears, and a moment's blackness in the face. The boy had never before tasted brandy pure, that was evident, and Joe perceived it.

"Jem," said he, "you've given the boy too much : you'll make him drunk—and then wot'll be the use on him ? "

" Nonsense ! " said Jem ; " it'll warm him, and give him pluck, poor little devil. Come along, my hearty."

And, seizing him by the one hand, whilst Joe grasped the other, they walked forward, the spaniel following them close behind.

The shadows thrown by the moon were curious ; on each side two big men, with points sticking out from each shoulder—for thus the moon sketched their guns ; and in the middle a little form, dwarfed yet more by the contrast on either side, his legs moving with great rapidity to keep up with the strides of his companions. Four smaller legs, and the movements of a tail that occasionally wagged were also visible on the white road. This was the spaniel.

They continued walking on for some time in silence ; the man named Jem occasionally turning round to see if the dog followed them. At last they came to a cross road, where they turned off abruptly to the left ; and after a further walk of some five minutes' duration, they suddenly stopped before a five-barred gate painted white, and overshadowed on either side by a row of tall and majestic elm-trees.

Jem placed his gun in his companion's hand, and climbed over the gate. When on the other side, he whispered, "Hand the youngster over." And in a moment Freddy was seized by Joe, and half thrown—as if he had been a doll, into the extended hands of Jem. Then the guns were handed over, and Joe proceeded to follow them. With a faint whistle to the dog, who leaped over one of the lower bars, they resumed the order of their march—Freddy between them—and pushed forward in silence. The trees began now to close around them; and in a short while they found themselves in a moderately thick wood.

" This will do, Joe?" said Jem, still in a whisper.

Then turning to Freddy, he said, " Now, look here, youngster,—you stand here, and keep your eyes and ears open. If you hear the least noise, blow the whistle I guv you. But mind, don't blow unless there's cause for it. Do yer understand?"

" Yes," said Freddy.

" And mind, again," said Jem, changing the tone of his voice, and speaking fiercely, " don't

move from here, or go to sleep. If I come back
and catch you gone, I'll kill yer; and if you're
asleep when we return—wot shall we do to him,
Joe?"

"Take him back to Fernley," said Joe.

"Ah! we'll take yer back to Fernley;—so
now you understand! But if you do your
duty, we'll be kind to yer:—we'll give yer a
supper and a bed, and lots of things you can't
guess at now."

But the threats were quite enough for Freddy.
Jem thought that his promise to slay him was
the most fearful; but Jem was mistaken: the
threat of being taken back to Fernley was infinitely more awful.

It was dark, but not completely so. The moon
was at its height now; and its rays, concentrated
by their vertical position, penetrated so far the
labyrinth of foliage as to render visible the
trunks of the trees, and here and there the occasional outline of a branch. In some parts there
were openings; and the floods of moonlight here
presented a wild and lovely effect.

Freddy watched the receding forms of the two
men out of sight. Then he began to grow
frightened. This was as bad, in one sense, as

the little black bedroom at Mr. Jerkins's. But, then, here there was no Mr. Jerkins. It was an Inferno—at least to the boy; but then it was an Inferno without fire.

To his great alarm an overpowering feeling of drowsiness began to take possession of him. This of course was the result of his draught from Jem's flask, united to the weariness consequent upon the extraordinary fatigue and excitement of the past evening. But potent as was the desire for sleep, the threats of Jem were more so; he shrank from even seating himself, and remained standing, rubbing his eyes hard to prevent them from closing.

Fate surely never accumulated a greater series of hardships upon any child than upon Freddy!

Five minutes had elapsed since the departure of the two men. Still Freddy remained standing, always rubbing his eyes, and always on the alert for the least noise in order that he might know when to sound upon the whistle. Doubtless this strained attention prevented him from falling down asleep.

All at once he heard at a distance the report of a gun: then another. Then there came a pause.

Presently a noise like the crackling of under-wood was audible, apparently approaching from the quarter in which the two men had disap-peared. Three or four moments after, a man came wildly rushing towards the spot where Freddy was standing; but before he reached it he threw his arms up in the air, staggered, and then fell headlong down upon the sward. At the same instant a large dog bounded out of the darkness, sniffed at the prostrate form of the man: then seeing Freddy, rushed at him and knocked him down. After which it placed one of its paws upon the boy's breast, and pro-ceeded to utter a series of long and dismal howls.

This dog had evidently great sagacity; but not of a sufficiently acute nature to perceive the inutility of keeping its paw upon the breast of an unconscious boy. Certainly, the sudden fright and fall would have bereft a strong man of his senses.

Guided by the outcries of the dog, a group of men, of whom one held a lantern, made their way slowly towards the spot.

This group consisted of five persons; one of whom was manacled ¡by the wrists, and his arms were clutched by a man on each side of him.

As they approached the prostrate form upon the sward, one of them stooped down, and holding the lantern close tu its head, turned the body over.

"He is dead," said a voice. "Here's where the shot went;" and a finger pointed to a black mark in the dead man's forehead.

"How could he have run so far with a bullet through his skull?" inquired another voice.

"Any other man would have dropped on the spot," said one of the five; "but poachers ain't men."

"That's a lie!" exclaimed the manacled man. "My pal Jem was as good as any on yer here. One by one he'd have licked you all. But damn yer, for a set of cowards! shootin' a man through the head behind his back!"

"Another lie for you!" said a voice. "If he wor shot behind, that mark wouldn't ha' been there!" and a finger pointed to the black mark indicated before.

"I don't care where ye shot him. He didn't see yer—and it wor all the same!"

"Shut up!" said one who grasped the man;

"none of your sauce here. You'd have killed us, if we hadn't shot him and caught you."

The dog, who during this conversation had ceased howling, suddenly recommenced.

" Hallo !" said the man who held the lantern, "there's Tiger! and who has he got under him ? "

He approached the dog, and the lantern threw a glare upon the features of the senseless boy.

"Hallo! there was three of 'em !" said the man.

"He's innocent," exclaimed the captive, suddenly; "I swear he's innocent ! We found him lyin' on the road-side, and my pal brought him along to keep watch. The youngster knew nothink of us, and we knew nothink of him."

" He's a pretty boy," said the man, scrutinising Freddy's features by the light of the lantern. "But how can I believe you ? "

" Believe me or not, I swear it's the truth. Wait till he comes to, and then question him. Don't go and lug him up along with me ! he ain't fit for such company, and wot's more, he's innocent—ay, as innocent as the babe unborn." And he concluded his speech with an energetic oath.

" Well, carry the prisoner off," said he of the lantern, who seemed to exercise a certain authority over the others; " I'll look after this youngster. When you've locked him up, come back for the dead one." Somebody said " All right," and the party moved off.

The bearer of the lantern having whistled off the dog, who proved to be a superb mastiff, stooped down and raised the boy in his arms. Next he pointed to the lantern, which the dog seized in its teeth by the ring; and with the four-legged torch-bearer in front to illumine his path, the man clasping the child, whose uncovered head rested upon his shoulders, moved slowly off in the direction of a light, which twinkled far down a long, though narrow avenue of trees.

CHAPTER IX.

THE GAMEKEEPER AND HIS WIFE.

On arriving at the cottage the man raised the latch of the door softly, and entered a small room lighted by a lamp at one end. Then placing the boy carefully down upon a short hair-cushioned sofa, he trod lightly towards another door and faintly tapped.

"Sarah!" cried he in a whisper.

"Yes?" answered a female voice from within.

"Oh! you're awake!" said the man, raising his voice. "Just come here, Sarah; I've got something to show you."

After a little the door was opened, and a woman came out in a flannel nightgown. A buxom, fair, and charming little woman she was! with eyes that looked black, and hair that seemed yellow in the light of the lamp. She threw her arms around her husband's neck and embraced him.

"Oh, I'm so glad you have come back," said she; "'I've only been in bed half an hour; and all that while I've been lying broad awake thinking of you and the poachers."

The husband, who was a remarkably fine specimen of an English yeoman—that is to say, possessing a good-humoured and intelligent British face, bushy black whiskers, broad shoulders, and one of those hands which you instinctively feel will give you a hearty shake—returned his wife's salute with great tenderness.

"We've had a bit of a tussle, you know," said he. "Did you hear the shots?"

"No."

"Yes, we let into 'em. One we've left clean dead."

Sarah turned pale, and clasped her hands together. "Oh, how dreadful!" she said. "Thank God, William, you're safe!"

"Look there, Sarah," said William, pointing to Freddy, who lay upon the sofa.

Sarah looked, and then uttered an exclamation of surprise. "Where did you find him?" she said.

"In the wood," replied William.

"But who does he belong to?"

"That's more than I know; we must wait until he wakes up. Ain't he a pretty child?"

Whilst he spoke Sarah had gone over to the boy and was bending down, examining him with mingled admiration and surprise. Suddenly she looked up to her husband, and in a frightened voice said,—

"William, this child isn't asleep: he's dead!"

"Dead!" cried William, running to her side, and taking Freddy's hand in his; then after a bit he said, "No, he ain't dead: he's in a swoon. I know what it was. Tiger knocked him down and frighted him."

"Let's undress him, and I'll put him into the bed," exclaimed Sarah.

Then seating herself, she took the boy upon her lap, his arms hanging apparently lifeless by his side, and his head lolling over her arm, and commenced taking off his clothes.

"I'm sure he's dead," said she, in a tremulous voice.

"I hope not," replied the husband.

"Oh, William, how awful it 'll be if he is."

"But he isn't, Sarah. I'm very sure of it; why, feel his hand—it's warm."

"That's true," said his wife.

"He's in a swoon," continued William. "I'll get a little vinegar and bathe his head."

"You'll find the cruet-stand in the cupboard. And William, while you are up, just go into the bedroom, and you'll see hanging up against the door a flannel gown. Bring it in, and I'll wrap him up in it. But don't make a noise, for Willie's asleep."

The husband, having executed these missions, knelt down by the side of the boy, and proceeded to bathe the little brow in some vinegar and water, which he had prepared in a bowl.

Meanwhile Sarah was rapidly undressing him, stripping him of his shoes and stockings and under-clothes, and chafing the little wearied limbs with her soft hands in a manner that sufficiently proclaimed her not to be altogether ignorant of the management of children.

After a little, Freddy gave signs of returning consciousness; his eyelids trembled, he gave a faint sigh, and a cold tremor ran through the light form.

"Why you're right, I declare, William," cried Sarah, in a delighted voice, enveloping the boy in the flannel gown, and propping his head with her arm.

"I was certain of it," said William, wisely smiling at his own penetration. "Now, if you'll take my advice, you'll put him at once to bed. In five minutes time we'll bathe his head again, and in the morning you'll have him all right, or my name's not William Smalter."

Saying which William Smalter took a pipe from the mantelpiece, and having filled it, commenced smoking with much pomp of demeanour.

Sarah raised the child carefully in her arms and William went before her, holding the lamp in his hand, to light her into the bedroom. Then she approached the bed, and turning down the coverlid, placed the boy, snugly wrapped in the flannel gown, in the exact indent made by her during that half hour before mentioned.

This being done, she softly stole round to the other side of the bed, and clasping her hands, looked down with eyes full of love upon something that was invisible to William where he stood. The husband noting this, laid down his pipe and crept round to his wife, leaning his chin upon her shoulder, and likewise looking down with a mouth that was broadened in a happy grin, and eyes that glistened with affection.

In a little cot before them slumbered an infant,

apparently some eighteen months or two years of age. Its plump little happy face, with eyelids closed in a profound sleep, peeped out from under the coverlid ; a fat and dimpled arm was thrown out on a line with its face, upon which its cheek reclined ; and one leg bent beneath the clothes marked with a very fair precision the outline and length of the concealed form. This was Willie.

At this moment Freddy gave a cry ; Sarah ran to the bed, and perceived his eyes wide open, staring at her with an amazed look. "Well, how do you do feel, my child ? " she asked him.

"Where am I ? " he said, faintly.

"Never mind now," she answered ; "to-morrow we will tell you all about it."

Freddy's eyes went wandering about the room ; at last he murmured, "I am so thirsty."

"That's a good sign," said William. "Sarah, I'll go and make him some tea. And I tell you what, you be spreading a little bed on the floor, where he can sleep to-night : or stay, the sofa 'll be better, eh ? "

"I think it will," replied Sarah.

In a moment William had grasped the sofa, and had placed it alongside the bed. Then he went into the other room and ignited a spirit-lamp, from which, after a little, there issued sounds as of water boiling,—noises that rendered evident the fact that Freddy's tea was in preparation.

By the time William's concoction was ready Sarah had finished the bed upon the sofa.

"Now," said she to Freddy, "put your arms around my neck, and I'll lift you into it."

Certainly, Freddy's arms had never before circled so soft a neck, nor his form pressed so gentle a bosom. The pretty little woman's eyes and smile had inspired him at once with a feeling of security and peace; but, too languid and ill from his past unnatural exertion, he could not even smile, but obeyed Sarah in silence, who raised him from her bed and tucked him up in his new, but not less comfortable, couch. Then she gave him a cup of tea, which he grasped and drank with avidity; after which he fell back, and, in a few minutes, was asleep.

The next morning, Freddy was awakened by somebody kissing him, and, on opening his eyes, he perceived Sarah standing by his side, holding a child in her arms. "My little Willie wanted to kiss you," she said. "Look, he's making

mouths at you again : he wants you to kiss him."
Freddy sat up, and threw his arms around the
neck of the infant, whose large eyes were survey-
ing him with a most friendly stare.

"And how do you feel now ? " asked Sarah.

"I've got a pain here," answered Freddy, pointing to his knees and thighs.

"Ah, it is rheumatism,—you have caught cold.
You mustn't get up to-day."

"Very well, mam," said Freddy, meekly.

"What a well-behaved little child ! " thought
Sarah. Then she added aloud, "I am going to
make your breakfast for you. If you like, I'll
put you into the big bed, and little Willie shall
keep you company ; unless, perhaps, you'd like
to go to sleep again ? " But Freddy had had
quite enough sleep.

"Oh please," said he, "let me have that little
boy to play with ! "

"Very well, you shall." Then smoothing down
the bed a-bit, she put Freddy into it, and, taking
off Willie's shoes, slipped him in by his side.
"Now," said she, "be careful to keep the clothes
well over you, and I'll go and make you a nice
basin of bread and milk." Saying which, with a
friendly nod and a smile, she left the room, taking

care, however, to leave the door open, in order
to keep an eye upon Willie, whom she feared
might, perhaps, in his ecstasy at the companionship of his new friend, roll himself out of
bed.

Ah, these were blissful hours for poor Freddy!
To his young heart, long accustomed to harsh-
ness, ill-usage, and every restraint that severity
or brutality can impose upon a young nature,
this was a heaven rendered more delicious by the
hell he had so lately left. How different was this
nice large bed from the little black hole at Mr.
Jerkins's! How different the sweet smell coming
in from the slightly-opened window, looking out
on to a blue sky and a smiling country, from the
musty, close rooms at Fernley, or the mustier,
sickly effluvium of the linen-draper's shop! And
how different the smiling little creature at his
side from the freckled, red-headed young Jerkinses, with their coarse language and coarser
manners! And *how* different this little, smiling,
pretty Sarah, from the gaunt, vulgar Mrs. Jerkins, or from the severe, acid, reserved, man-
woman, Miss Godstone!

Freddy had never had a companion before:
hence little Willie was treated by him as only

infancy long accustomed to loneliness can treat
its first friend. Very entertaining would it un-
questionably have been to the benevolent observer
of human nature in its first stage, to have watched
these two children together. Now that Sarah was
absent, the restraint that even she could not help
exercising over the stranger, Freddy, passed
away; and though still feeble, and far from well,
he gave loose to every impulse of his young nature, and laughed, and talked, and tickled his
friend to his heart's content. Nor was little
Willie at all behind him in this spontaneous
familiarity. He kicked his fat legs up in the
air; he threw his arms round Freddy's neck and
kissed him; he prattled in a language unintelligible to all but the attentive ear of the listening
mother without; he ducked his head under the
clothes, and cooed away, pretending to have hidden, and when he reappeared he would roll over
upon Freddy, and bury his face in his neck, literally screaming with joy.

Who shall describe the inward contentment of
the mother who occasionally popped her head
in at all this? Her husband had left early: he
was head-gamekeeper to Sir William Marrison,
upon whose estate his cottage was built; and she

longed for his return, to say, " The two children
do get on so well together ! "

When, however, he *did* come in—which occurred at one o'clock, that being his dinner-time,—
she told him, and he seemed to listen to her with
much satisfaction.

" Do you think he's well enough for me to talk
with him ? " he asked.

" Well, you might try," answered Sarah ; " you
can always give over, should he be too weak."

" For you know," said William, " I should like
to find out something about him. He seems a
very gentleman-like boy, don't he ? "

" Ay, that he does, and is," said Sarah ;
" he's as polite as possible, and always calls
me mam."

" Does he now ? " said the gratified husband.
" Well, now, I call that very nice and well-bred
of him."

" And so do I, William."

" Is he in bed now ? " demanded William.

" Yes."

" Is Willie with him ? "

" He is ; but I'll go in and fetch him out."

" Ah, do ; I can talk to him then freer-
like."

The younger of the bedded couple rather objected to being taken away. He had been with
Freddy the whole morning, and was as comfortable as possible, not having the least desire to
quit his warm premises. Indeed, he had reckoned
upon being left there the whole day; for besides
the immense advantage it afforded him of having
constantly by his side an amiable and pretty play-
fellow, he found that he was enabled to enjoy a
double repast, as experience had already assured
him. Besides his own breakfast, which he had
had before Freddy was awake, he participated
also largely in the basin of bread and milk with
which Freddy had been that morning regaled.

I do not think it necessary to repeat the conversation that ensued ,between William and his
young guest. In substance, Freddy's revelations
were exactly those which M. Gautier had gathered
from him, though to William, of course, there was
a good deal more to tell. It was not, however,
without much hesitation that Freddy brought
himself to confess that he had run away from
Fernley; nor was the expression on William's
face that heralded this disclosure at all reassur-
ing. But when Freddy told him his motive for
this sudden departure; when he had acquainted

him in his childish, though not less convincing, way of the circumstances of the whole affair; of the character of the Jerkinses; of the treatment, disposition, and the threats of the linen-draper, and the many other lesser circumstances connected with his short sojourn at Fernley; the whole matter then assumed a totally different complexion. With a sagacity that did credit to him, the gamekeeper perceived at once the truthfulness of the boy's narrative, wondered no longer at the child whom he had, since meeting him, secretly considered as a very great mystery, but, slapping his own leg violently, swore that had he been in Freddy's place he would have done exactly the same thing; and declared that if ever fate should so arrange the order of things as to bring him in collision with Mr. Jerkins, he would inflict upon him such punishment as would make him remember to his dying day, not only the instrument of his retribution, but the cause of it as well.

This is in effect (though not precisely the terms of) what Mr. William Smalter said and swore; and, having concluded his emphatic and violent declamation, he called out to his wife, and bade her come in to hear Freddy's story, which he asked him to repeat, commencing from his first recollection of Miss Godstone, and ending at the moment when he was knocked down senseless by the mastiff, Tiger.

"I do declare," said Sarah, when Freddy had once more arrived at a conclusion, "I do declare to you, William, that I do believe some folks are born without hearts at all. I don't mean the thing that bobs up and down inside one, but what people call heart, which I take to mean kindness, and a will to give when something's wanted and something is to be given."

"You're quite right, Sarah. Some folks, as you say, haven't more heart in 'em than my boot, no, nor that pipe, nor anything else that can't feel. Well, he shan't go back to Fernley, shall he? nor to his aunt's, neither?"

"No, that he shan't."

Freddy gave them both a smile, so full of gratitude, that Mrs. Sarah could not contain herself, but got up and heartily embraced him. Seeing which, and probably thinking himself called upon to follow her example, William rose and did the same thing. Then little Willie was put again by his side, and the worthy gamekeeper and his wife left the room, perfectly satisfied with Freddy's tale, and growing every instant more attached to him.

The time passed very pleasantly with Freddy now. He soon recovered his lost health, and grew possessed of a flow of spirits that he had never experienced before. Day by day he was fast losing that air of timidity, that nervous start when suddenly accosted,—in a word, those thousand little emotions which characterise the child long used to tyranny, and which, to Freddy, had been a portion of his character. This young flower, nipped so long by the cold blasts of unkindness and even cruelty, in the sunlight of this more congenial clime assumed all its native loveliness. The bloom of health sat upon his cheek, and the light of young gladness rendered brilliant his eye. In Willie he had found a companion, and the void in the boy's heart was filled. True, one of an age more approaching his would have been better adapted to him; but in this child, who was at least a quiet, good little thing, he was possessed of a playmate,—someone who would join him in chasing a ball, in pursuing a hoop, in gathering flowers by the hedgerow; and this is what children pine for in loneliness; and this is what Freddy had never known until now.

But then, Willie was not his only companion. For the good-natured, smiling, pretty little mother was as much a child as either of them; and would take them out into the fields and romp with them until want of breath forced them to romp no longer. Moreover, the gamekeeper would make kites and fly them, to the inexpressible gratification of Freddy, who had never before seen such a spectacle, and who, therefore, at the first one that went up, gave vent to his amazement in a loud cry of wonder. Mr. Smalter would also, sometimes, take him out for a walk in the grounds and park belonging to the estate; and once, just as they turned a path leading into a meadow, they met the proprietor, Sir William Marrison, an old man, with a benevolent smile. The gamekeeper touched his cap, and the baronet, pointing to the boy, said, " Why, Smalter, I thought you had only one child ? "

" That's all I have, sir," answered Smalter.

" But I thought he was quite young ? " said the baronet.

" So he is, sir," answered Smalter; " but this isn't my child."

" Why, whose is he, then ? "

Smalter told his master the story, and when he had concluded, Sir William said to him, " Have you been keeping him at your own expense all this time ? "

" Why, yes, Sir William."

" It's very generous of you," said Sir William ; " very. I am always pleased at an action of this sort. Here, put this guinea in the lad's pocket : it may be of use to him some day; and as for you, next pay-day don't forget to remind me to add to your wages a five-pound note, do you hear ? "

" Ah, Sir William, you are too good ! May God bless and spare you for many a long year to come."

" Benevolence is scarce in this world, Smalter, and when I meet with it I always endeavour to reward it. Good morning."

" Good morning, Sir William, and may God bless you."

" Good morning, my little man ! "

And nodding with a kind smile at Freddy, the old baronet walked slowly on.

" Who's that good gentleman ? " asked the boy.

" That's my master," said Smalter, proudly.

"May I put the money on this?" asked Freddy, drawing out the guard attached to the little medal given to him by Rosalie, and which he had worn round his neck ever since it had been placed there by the young French girl.

"It'll alter its value if I go piercing it," said Smalter; "and every mite may be of service to you some day."

The boy appeared to reflect for a moment, and then said, "Oh, very well: I will keep it here," and he slipped it into his pocket.

"Be careful you don't lose it," said Smalter; "it's lots of money, and will buy heaps of things."

"Oh, I'll be very careful," said Freddy.

Time passed. The summer wore away; the winter came on; Freddy still lived with the gamekeeper and his wife, heedless of the future, happy in the present, almost forgetful of the past.

One day Smalter went out as usual in the morning, and his wife set about making breakfast for the children and preparing for the other household duties of the day. He had hardly been gone half an hour, when Willie, who stood at the window cried out, "Oh! there's father." These were words he had learnt to say with distinctness.

Sarah looked out and perceived her husband coming down the walk, his manner dejected, his whole demeanour one of distress. He entered the cottage, and flinging himself down upon a chair, leant his head upon his hand. "Why, what's the matter, William?" asked his wife, anxiously.

"Oh Sarah!" exclaimed the gamekeeper.

She ran towards him and bending down looked closely into his face. "Are you not well?" she asked.

"Thank God, yes. But oh! Sarah, Sir William Marrison's dead!"

"Dead!" cried Sarah.

"Yes, he died this morning at four o'clock. Oh dear, what a blow!"

Sarah bowed her head with a gesture full of sorrow.

"The property 'll be sold and cut up into lots for building. I'm certain of this, for it's been a long time talked of, only Sir William said it should never be while he lived. But now it all comes to his son who's a merchant down in London, and who has an estate in Kent. He won't want this, and it 'll be cut up into lots and sold. Then there 'll be no use of me!"

Poor Sarah was utterly overwhelmed by this news. "And shall we have to leave here?" she cried.

"Yes, certain. I'm going to-day to look out for a gardener's place at once. I'm too poor to live in idleness."

Such was the stroke of Fate, that like an avalanche came tumbling down about the heads of this honest couple, burying them for awhile in a world of woe. But every good man's heart is a sun, before which these avalanches, if they are allowed time, will gradually dissolve. Such a sun-like heart had William Smalter.

"I'm thinking now of the child, Sarah," said he, as the two sat conversing together in the evening; "I can't afford to keep him, you know— and I won't turn him adrift."

"Turn him adrift!" cried Sarah, "No, indeed! rather than that I'd go out and beg in the streets."

"Haven't you got a cousin, or an aunt, or somebody, living in London in the bookselling line?"

"To be sure I have; it's a cousin and his name's Smugg."

"Ah, Smugg! I remember now. Don't you

think they'll take Freddy if you was to ask
them?"

"Yes! I'm sure they would! that's a beautiful thought. I haven't seen Charley Smugg for
six years—no, for five years come June next.
Then he was as nice a man as you could wish to
meet. He was an old suitor of mine, William."

"Was he?" said William, frigidly.

"Yes, and he liked me too, William."

"Did he!" muttered William.

"He would have married me," continued the
little woman, musingly, "only mother thought
he didn't promise so flourishing as he's turned
out to be."

"Humph!" said William.

"But then *you* came, William," said the little
woman; "*you* came, and after I had seen you I
never thought anything more of poor Charley
Smugg."

"And now," said William, gratified by the
avowal, "you'd better write the letter."

It took a long time to write; for, ably as Sarah
performed all other vocations, letter-writing was
certainly not her forte. Nor did she get much
help from her husband, who sat with one finger

out, dictating; for this was all he could do. But then his dictation was infinitely more perplexing than his silence would have been. He said such a deal, and this, too, in such a roundabout manner, that had Sarah written all that fell from his mouth, not twenty large folio sheets would have contained it.

But everything must sooner or later come to an end; and as Sarah's letter was not exempt from this rule, it came at last to the part which seemed to her the least difficult—signing her name. Then the paper was folded up and addressed, ready for the early post on the following morning, and our couple went to bed.

The answer arrived two days after. It was satisfactory, merely expressing a reasonable doubt at the capabilities of the young person for his office as a species of clerk in a small bookseller's shop. But Mrs. Smalter replied, that she would guarantee the boy she recommended; for, said she, he is clever, polite, willing, and active, writes a good hand, that only wants practice to render beautiful. So the matter was settled; and then came the disagreeable duty of acquainting Freddy with the arrangement that had taken place for him, and the necessity for his parting with the family.

What he felt it is not easy to describe. He greeted this communication first with incredulity, then with amazement, and lastly with a paroxysm of weeping. In vain Mr. Smalter told him he was going to London to be made a man of; he declared he didn't want to be a man at all. In vain he was informed that a colossal fortune might be his at no distant time. Had he but had the language to express himself, he would assuredly have answered that money was dross; that he thirsted not for wealth; that he only wanted to remain where he was.

At last, Mr. Smalter, whose heart inwardly bled at the boy's grief, but who fought hard to conceal his emotion, determined to try another tack. So taking the boy on his lap, he pointed out to him that he (Mr. Smalter) was poor; that he could not support him; that it would be a struggle now even to maintain the two who were dependent on him. · This, spoken in language adapted to his understanding, seemed to make an impression upon him. He ceased his passionate weeping, and though his sobs occasionally burst forth it was apparent that he was endeavouring to subdue them. Mr. Smalter tapped him on the back, and called him a brave lad! a man! a warrior!

It was arranged that Mr. Smugg should pay the expenses of his clerk's travelling. This was a great relief to poor Mr. Smalter, who could have ill-afforded the eleven and three-pence.

The day of parting at last came, and amidst a perfect storm of weeping, Freddy was conveyed to the coach that passed along the high road— that road upon whose wayside Freddy had less than a year ago been found asleep—that road which also led to Fernley. Ah! what a horrible road to be sure.

Mr. Smalter had been commissioned to see him off, Sarah not being quite certain as to how she might stand the parting. Nor would she let Willie go; for, she argued, and with justice, "The sight of him will be sure to make him take on bad again."

The two arrived at the corner of the road where the coach passed, and before long they heard the rattling of its wheels, and the tramp of its horses some distance off. All at once somebody raised a cry behind them, and turning round, they beheld Sarah running in their direction. She held something up in her hand, which looked like a piece of white paper.

As she approached them a piece of white paper it proved to be, though evidently it contained something.

" Oh," said Sarah, panting, "just in time! Poor boy; he had nearly forgotten his guinea. Willie only this moment saw it on the mantelpiece."

Freddy hung down his head, but refused to take it from the hand that was proffering it.

" Why," said Mr. Smalter, " what, won't you take it ? "

Still silent. The coach was now approaching them ; in a few moments it would draw up.

" Quick ! cried Mr. Smalter, " take it—we shan't have any time—here."

Freddy burst out crying, and amidst his sobs, exclaimed, " I don't want it—I left it behind for you—I don't want it, indeed, I don't."

Poor little fellow! it was all he had to give, and this he gave. Sarah stooped down hurriedly and kissed him, and blinded with her tears, went stumbling towards her little home.

Smalter said nothing; but his glistening eyes sufficiently proclaimed his feelings. He thrust the money into the boy's pocket, and taking him by the hand, walked towards the coach that had now drawn up.

The boy carried his wardrobe in an old leathern-bag belonging to Sarah. Its contents consisted of a shirt, cut out of an old article of a similar nature, belonging to Smalter; some socks, knitted by the little woman; one or two pocket-handkerchiefs, made out of heaven knows what! and fashioned heaven knows how! and a few other small articles, all the handicraft of the industrious and benevolent Sarah!—God will reward thee, Sarah!—in this bag was also concealed a plum cake! Ah, Sarah! Sarah!

" Take care of him!" cried Smalter to the guard.

" Ay! ay!" answered the guard.

" God bless you, Freddy!"

Smalter stood waving his hand: the guard gave a signal; the horses were instantly put into a trot, and in a few moments the coach had disappeared round an angle of the road.

END OF BOOK II.

BOOK III.

BOOK III.

———•———

CHAPTER I.

A PIECE OF VILLANY.

On the 22nd of May, 1852, the ship "Water-Witch," from Hong Kong to London, was lying becalmed between the islands of Java and Sumatra.

As all the world very well knows, either by experience or by the map, the straits between these two coasts are very narrow; so much so, indeed, that the land on either side seems perpetually ahead, as if about to close on you, though this is a mere delusion of the eye. Nevertheless, this makes these straits very formidable to navigate; and generally, when ships are caught here in a calm, they will either furl or clew up their sails and drop anchor, so as to avoid being carried by the currents into dangerous proximity with the land.

VOL. II. H

Though the "Water-Witch" was, in one
sense, becalmed, she had all her sails still
spread ; and as the faintest air will give a vessel
steerage-way, there was just wind enough abroad
to prevent the "Water-Witch" from yielding
entirely to the currents.

It was the hour of sunset. Though the line of
coast on the starboard side of the ship rendered
invisible the sinking orb of day, the whole of
the evening sky above was superb in those
manifold colours, which, commencing with
purple and gold, gradually fade away eastward
in a blue dark, liquid and profound—alike,
marking the departure of day, and the approach
of night. Against this superb background the
outline of the land was sharply defined ; sometimes leaping into angular projections, sometimes
smooth and straight as the horizon. On the
other side, visible on the port-bow of the ship,
could be seen rising from behind a Lilliputian
promontory, the tapering masts and spars of
some half-dozen vessels, marking the spot where
was situated the little Dutch settlement called
Batavia.

On board the "Water-Witch" all was still.
Many of the crew were upon deck, standing or

sitting, in evident expectation of being soon called to bring the ship to an anchor; but they conversed in subdued voices, awed at once by the beauty of the surrounding scene, and by the presence of the captain and officers, who were walking up and down 'aft upon the poop. One voice alone broke this general stillness; it was the sailor who stood in the main-chains, crying out at intervals the number of fathoms he had sounded with the lead.

The captain was a beef-faced, short man, with bow-legs, and wearing a hat upon his head. Yet, in spite of this, a thorough sailor, as you could perceive by the manner in which he looked about him, or up at the cloud of canvas above, which a word from his mouth would melt into long black stripes.

"We shall get the evening-breeze down from the land, sir, I suspect, before eight bells," said the chief-mate.

"I don't think so, Mr. Saunders," said the captain. "The weather looks settled, and I think we had better take in sail before it grows dark."

"Very well, sir."

"Is the chain-cable ready for'ard?"

"Yes, sir."

"Then bring the ship to."

"Ay, ay, sir."

In a moment the mate had advanced to the brass-railing overlooking the quarter-deck, and with both hands to his face had bellowed out his orders. Instantly came the shrill whistle of the boatswain's pipe, and then all was hurry, bustle, and confusion. The vast stretch of canvas, that had but a few minutes before reared itself majestically aloft, vanished; a number of dark figures were seen running up the rigging, and at the same moment a heavy splash, accompanied by the hoarse rattle of a massive chain, told the uninitiated that the "Water-Witch" was at anchor.

In a quarter of an hour's time all was again silent. The men had disappeared in the fore-castle, and were now busily employed in getting their tea. Three persons alone were visible 'aft; one was the captain, who had lighted a cigar, and who was walking up and down by him-self near the wheel; another, one of the mates, was pacing the deck to and fro on the fore-part of the poop; and the last, a tall figure, evidently a passenger, stood looking over the ship's side at the water, that gurgled and occasionally flashed below.

He stood for some minutes thus, motionless, absorbed in a profound reverie. Then raising his head, he perceived the captain walking by himself, and went over to him. It was now growing rapidly dark ; the last flake of the sun-set had disappeared, and the sky was gemmed with stars. In these latitudes night immediately follows the departure of the sun ; there is no twilight.

"Good evening, captain."

"Ah, good evening, Mr. Belmont. Here we are—stuck, you see."

"I hope not for long, captain ; heaven knows, the voyage is long enough, without need of any further protraction by calms."

"You're right," said the captain. "But don't fear ; I've wagered to be in the London Docks before the end of August, and, please the pigs, I'll be there."

"Your ship is a fine sailer ; she hasn't been long doing the run from Hong Kong here, has she ? And that speaks well for the future—at least, when she gets the monsoons and the trade-winds."

" She's the fastest craft on the line," said the captain, proudly; " only give her wind, she wants nothing more."

" Does she beat the 'Jasper'? " asked Belmont.

" The 'Jasper'! " exclaimed the captain, with contempt. " Why, sir, the 'Witch' would draw a wake around her, and then be out of sight before she could get clear of it! "

" I'm sorry for that; for I've consigned some goods to London by the 'Jasper,' and I am anxious that she shouldn't be delayed."

" Ah, then, you haven't given us all, Mr. Belmont! " said the captain, in a slightly mortified tone.

" You should have had it, captain," answered Belmont; " but Swann, the 'Jasper's' skipper, you know, is an old friend of mine—at least, I've known him ever since I've been in Hong Kong; and one likes to serve a friend now and then."

" That's true," said the captain. Then, after a pause, he said, " I suppose you're returning to Hong Kong again, next year ? "

" No," said Belmont, " I have bid adieu to it for ever."

" For ever ! " exclaimed the captain. " Oh,

don't say that, Mr. Belmont. What'll the London merchants do without you?"

"As they did before, I suppose," answered Belmont, laughing. "I have made my little money, and now I am anxious to return to old England."

"And enjoy life, Mr. Belmont, eh? Well, I can't blame you. I wish I could do the same thing. By the way, you've got no' reason to quarrel with Fortune; for, let me see, you haven't been in Hong Kong for more than—how long, Mr. Belmont?"

"About six years."

"Ay—I was going to say—for I've been in this trade twelve, and don't remember you much before five years ago. Well, a man who can come out from England, and make his fortune in six years, I call deuced lucky."

"So he is; only I didn't come from England first. The foundation of my present success was laid in Australia."

"The diggings; for that's what everybody begins with?"

"No, I squatted."

"Ah, sheep, hey?" cried the captain. "Well, I've always thought there was nothing like squatting to make a fortune on. If a man isn't too proud to work hard for the first year or two in a strange country, he'll be sure to get on."

" Your assurance is my experience. You are quite right."

" I suppose then, Mr. Belmont, you have sold your business at Hong Kong ? "

" In one sense, yes; I have been bought out."

" Handsome, of course ? " said the captain.

" Come, captain, you are growing inquisitive," said Belmont, good-naturedly.

" Ha ! ha ! " laughed the captain. " So I am. But we're a blunt lot, we old sea-fogies, Mr. Belmont, and not over particular in our behaviour as a rule. You see how I can sit upon my own business—ha ! ha ! But I hope you haven't thought me rude, sir, in my questions ? "

" Not at all—not at all. On the contrary. I like a talkative man, for he's generally good society. He may be a bore sometimes ; but with all his faults, he's worth fifty thousand of your sombre men, who muffle themselves up in a cold and reserved demeanour, frigidly or curtly answering when they are addressed—and that's all."

The captain might have thought Belmont

ironical; for, besides having acquired the precise character of the men he had himself just sketched in the society of Hong Kong, his conduct on board, from the time the ship had left port, by no means tended to belie in the captain's estimation the voice of fame.

But whatever the captain's private opinion might have been, he openly and heartily agreed in the truth of Belmont's remark—remarking, that he detested the cold, silent man, whom he always viewed with suspicion, as either meditating a crime or concealing a wrong. Then, catching a sight of the cabin through the grating of the sky-light, he said, " Hallo, it's ten o'clock ! the grog's on the table ; let's go down." He went towards the hatchway, and descended the steps, Belmont following him.

Two hours elapsed, and the night still remained dark and calm. As eight bells—namely, twelve o'clock—was being sounded, Belmont reappeared from the hatchway and stepped upon the deck. Nobody was visible, and advancing to the side of the ship, he leaned against the sail, and proceeded to puff in silence from a cigar which he held between his lips. He was enveloped in a warm cloak, though the night was far from cold;

so far, indeed, that he had found his little cabin too warm, and had come upon deck to breathe the fresh air, and to smoke his cigar in silence. The position he had assumed was uncomfortable, and he cast his eyes around him in search of a more convenient support. They alighted on the little hatchway, leading to the cabin. Advancing towards it, Belmont seated himself by its side, folding his arms, and leaning back, with his cloak wrapped round him, and his eyes fixed on the dark line of coast, rendered perceptible against its background of stars. Close beside him rose the mizenmast, throwing over him a deeper shadow yet than that already caused by the hatchway and the night.

He had not been seated long thus, before he heard the tread of some one coming along the deck, and a young man passed by without observing him. Belmont knew him to be the second-mate, who was now come to take the watch, but he did not care to accost him, preferring to be alone; and that the light of his cigar might not betray his presence, he concealed it, as the second mate passed, within the palm of his hand.

Meanwhile the young mate had gone round to

the other side of the deck, and was there walking up and down, with a light and regular tread.

With the exception of the sounds of these footsteps, the ship seemed buried in a profound stillness. The man on the look out on the forecastle, seeing the inutility of keeping watch, was lying with his head in a coil of rope asleep. In the forecastle itself, the heavy breathing that issued from the hammocks and the bunks, that were suspended or ranged round the ship's sides, rendered evident the presence of the drowsy god. In the after-cabin all the lights were out,—indeed, no light was anywhere visible, save one little lantern suspended near the main hatchway leading into the 'tween-decks, which, in the "Water Witch," had been loaded with cargo. But the space by which an entrance into the hold was to be gained was clear.

The coolness of the atmosphere, the silence of the night, the faint creaking of the cable caused by the current swaying the ship from the line of the anchor, all conspired to possess Belmont with a feeling of drowsiness; his head nodded upon his breast, and a few minutes more would infallibly have seen him asleep, when suddenly a noise caused him to start; he raised his head, and heard behind him the sounds of the voices of two men speaking together in a whisper.

Low as they spoke every word fell distinctly upon his ear. His first feeling had been to make some movement that they might become aware of his presence; but something that one of them was saying caused him to remain motionless, listening intently with bated breath and startled thoughts.

"All hands are asleep," said a voice, "and the light's out in the skipper's cabin; the man on the look-out is also asleep, and I think now's the time to do the job, as there aint no chance of our being disturbed."

"Have you got everything ready?" said the other voice, which Belmont recognised as the second-mate's. "Where's that twisting machine of yours?"

"Here."

There was a pause: it seemed as if some instrument were being inspected.

"You see," continued the other, "this is better than the chisel. We'd have wanted a hammer then, and the chances are we'd have been heard. Now, all that I have to do is to press this against the side and drive it round."

" Will it penetrate, do you think ? "

" Ay, the devil himself ! "

" All right," said the voice of the second-mate ; " come along ; we haven't any time to lose."

" Are the boats ready ? "

" Yes ; I saw to that myself this morning."

The voices ceased, and then came the light tread of two men walking away. Belmont raised his head, and perceived them descending the ladder leading on to the main-deck. Noiselessly rising, he followed them on tip-toe, bending double to avoid marking his figure against the star-lit sky. When he approached the ladder, he perceived the two men standing near the main hatchway,—a large square hole cut in the deck, which, first of all, leads (at least in large ships) into what is termed the 'tween-decks, and afterwards into the hold or bottom of the vessel ;— they were holding here a short conference, both of them glancing cautiously about them as they spoke. After awhile one turned, and, placing his foot on a ladder, proceeded to descend, the other following him. When they reached the lower deck, they unhooked the lantern, and, one of them stripping himself of his coat, enveloped the light in it.

Though ignorant of their purpose, Belmont was well aware that these men were bent upon some piece of villany. Still following them, be advanced on tip-toe round to the mainmast, and, hiding himself behind it, peered down into the hatchway beneath.

The lantern had been so muffled as to emit only a single ray, which the second-mate concentrated upon the staple of the iron bar that retained the lid of the hatchway in its position. Belmont observed that the other man was busily employed in drawing this staple out, pausing every now and then to listen, then resuming his occupation with intense eagerness. A satisfactory grunt at length pronounced this, evidently the most hazardous and difficult part of the business, to be accomplished. Then seizing the iron bar, the man noiselessly drew it out of the further staple, and carefully placed it down. The two men next proceeded to remove a portion of the tarpaulin, or tarred canvas-covering from the corner of the hatchway; and jerking, though always silently, one part of the grating or lid from its position, the hold stood open, blackly yawning beneath them.

The time occupied in this transaction was not

more than two minutes. A landsman would have bungled twice that number of hours over the same job.

The man, having placed his hands upon the edge of the hatchway, stooped down and lowered his legs and body into the blackness. Belmont imagined, for a moment, that if he should let go his hands now he would break his neck; but in this he was mistaken; for the man *did* let go his hands, but, instead of falling, remained where he was. It was evident his feet had found a support on a portion of the cargo.

The second-mate handed his associate the lantern, then followed him, taking care, however, to pull the tarpaulin covering over the hole.

What were they going to do?

Belmont left his hiding-place; but before descending into the hatchway, he removed his shoes. He understood that if these men's designs were criminal, the discovery of his presence might result in his murder.

He stole softly down and listened.

All was silent.

He raised a small corner of the tarpaulin and peeped into the darkness. For a moment he

neither saw nor heard anything. Suddenly, there
was a sound as of the movement of a box or case,
and all at once a bright light flashed against the
ship's side, some distance below the level upon
which he was kneeling, and six or eight yards
away from him. This irradiated the form of only
one man, who was kneeling, with his face towards
the side of the vessel. By his attitude it was
apparent he was leaning against some kind of
carpenter's tool, which, by the regular movement
of his arm, it seemed he was turning.

Like lightning the truth flashed upon the mind
of Belmont. They were boring a hole in the
vessel's side below the water-line !

They were scuttling the ship !

Hardly had this discovery been made before
Belmont was upon deck, and in a few seconds
after he had burst into the captain's cabin.

" Wake up ! wake up ! there are two men in
the hold scuttling your ship ! "

The captain, who had been aroused from a
dead sleep, had not heard what Belmont had
said. Knowing, however, by Belmont's aspect
that there was danger, and concluding, for a
moment, that it might be a storm, he hopped
out of his cot with the alacrity of a seaman,

shouting out, as he eagerly thrust his arms into his coat,—

"Let go the maintops'l hallyards! down with outer and inner jibs! let fly tacks and sheets!"

The worthy man had evidently, in his sudden alarm, forgotten two things: firstly, that he was in his cabin; secondly, that his ship was at anchor.

"Hush!" cried Belmont; and he rapidly repeated to him what he had witnessed.

"Are they still there?" half shrieked the captain.

"Yes!" was the answer.

Swift as thought the captain passed out of his cabin, and darted along the deck into the forecastle. He evidently knew what he was about now. Before twenty seconds had elapsed, he had thumped as many men out of their hammocks on to their feet; and in a very short while after, he was darting, at the head of some dozen men, in the direction of the hold.

Belmont was there waiting for them. He anticipated that the moment the two men below heard the tramp overhead, they would extinguish their light; and he had, therefore, snatched a swinging lamp from the captain's table, which he had ignited as he passed through the door. He thrust this into the hands of the foremost man who passed him, and then the whole twelve men poured into the hold, the captain standing at the edge of the hatch urging them on with cries and execrations.

The scene that ensued was truly ridiculous, in spite of the anything but funny cause that had provoked it. The captain had shouted to the men the facts of the case as they had been furnished him by Belmont; and the crew, who knew not but that it was the intention of the two men to sink the ship and all hands with her, were exasperated to the last degree. Moreover, curiosity urged them forward to discover who these two men were; for in the sudden rush they had not had time to notice who were present or who were absent. The tumultuous manner in which they fell, pell-mell, into the hold, though ludicrous enough, argued very well for their bravery. On they went, shouting, scrambling, sometimes grasping each other by mistake, and rolling in couples down between the interstices caused by the Chinese mode of packing casks or cases of tea. How they discovered the two men by the aid of such a feeble light as the little lantern afforded them, I cannot tell; but discover them they certainly did; for, after the scrambling, the shouting, and the grasping had been repeated many times over, a voice suddenly cried out, " Here's one of 'em; " and almost immediately after, another voice shouted, " And here's t'other! " Then a rush was made in the direction of the voices, and, strange to say, a fierce struggle took place. For, whether the two men, conscious that the penalty consequent upon the discovery of their atrocious attempt was, if not death, at least some punishment hardly less terrible, sought to anticipate their doom; or that rage at their ill-success and at the threats and execrations of their messmates goaded them to attempt the unequal conflict; it is certain that a fierce hand-to-hand struggle took place, a long time occurring before the two scoundrels were at length bound and hauled up upon deck.

The number of black eyes and bloody noses, of scraped shins and lacerated hands, was terrible. But the worst sufferers were the two men; the second-mate having his nose broken, his lips cut open, and his whole form fearfully bruised and shaken; whilst his companion, who proved to be the ship's carpenter, had received such terrible injuries about the breast and head, that hardly had he been laid upon the deck, and the surgeon called out to attend him, than his head fell back, and he expired.

The whole night was passed by the captain in rigidly scrutinising the ship's bottom, so fearful was he lest the miscreants might have so far succeeded in their attempt as to have made one hole. Fortunately for his ship she was built of teak, a wood through which it requires a longer time to drill a hole than had been allowed to the ship's carpenter.

Belmont was, of course, looked upon as having saved the vessel. He received the thanks of the whole ship's company, the captain and remaining officers, together with four or five passengers, agreeing to make up a purse for a testimonial to him when they reached England.

CHAPTER II.

A CONFESSION.

ONE day, about two weeks after they had left Java, the captain said to Belmont,—

"The second-mate that was is dying!"

"Poor wretch!" exclaimed Belmont; "what could have induced him to attempt so foul a crime as scuttling your ship?"

"That is just what puzzles me," said the captain. "I have tried to question him, but he won't answer. Well, his secret 'll have to go overboard with him, for the surgeon tells me he'll be dead before a week's gone."

"Is he in irons?"

"No; hang it! I can't keep a dying man in irons. I had them struck off this morning."

"Where is he confined?"

"In his cabin."

"Would I be allowed to see him? Perhaps I

should be more successful in gaining his secret from him."

" Yes; I don't suppose there'll be any harm in it. I've appointed the surgeon his jailer. He's the responsible party; so before I say yes, I'll just consult him about it."

Some hours later the captain said, "I have spoken to Wilkins, the surgeon, and he says you're quite welcome to visit his prisoner. I hope you'll be successful in worming the secret from him."

" I hope I shall," replied Belmont.

The second-mate's cabin was in the fore part of the cuddy, having a little window that looked on to the main-deck. This little window was closed now to prevent the encroaching stare of the idle or the curious about the deck. So also was the round porthole, which looked on to the sea; but this out of precaution, for they knew not but that the inmate of the cabin might anticipate his fate, by thrusting himself through it into the water. The door of the cabin was kept locked, and the key held by the surgeon, Mr. Wilkins, who opened it merely to feed the prisoner or ad-minister his doses.

" You'll find him stubborn, and, it seems to

me, thick-headed," said the surgeon, as he put the key into Belmont's hand. " Poor devil, I am really sorry for him ; for he is a young man, and an almost certain death awaits him in the course of a few days. The injuries on the chest and lungs are terrible, and every hour I expect to see symptoms of internal mortification taking place."

On opening the door, Belmont observed the young man lying on his back, in what seamen call " a bunk," that is to say, a sort of fixed cot nailed against the side of the cabin. His eyes were closed, his hair hung matted about his fore-head, and his thin, attenuated face wore an expression of intense suffering.

He opened his eyes as Belmont entered, but did not turn his head.

" I have come to see how you are," said Belmont ; " I should have been before, but I feared you might have considered my visit an intrusion."

" Oh, it is you, Mr. Belmont ? " said the prisoner, languidly.

" How do you feel now ? "

" Very, very ill, sir."

Too ill, Belmont plainly perceived, to be able to support the fatigue of a conversation.

"You must feel lonely here," said he, in a tone of commiseration; "would you like me to read to you a little ?" ·

"You are very kind, sir."

"What shall it be ?"

There was a pause; at length the sick man turning his head with a painful effort, whispered,—

"Have you the Bible, sir ?"

"No; but I will go and get one."

It may be necessary for me to say here that the prisoner was quite unconscious of Belmont having been the instrument of the discovery of his meditated crime. He had imputed it to accident,—to a want of precaution on his side; in a word, he believed the discovery to be owing entirely to the captain, who had come upon deck, and remarking his absence had searched for him.

Belmont soon returned, and seating himself by the side of the bed, proceeded to read aloud from the open volume on his knee.

He was a fine man with handsome features, rendered striking by their strong expression of intelligence. His forehead, which was lofty and possessing great breadth, was lightly traced with a series of lines—thin, almost imperceptible; visible, however, when he smiled, or when he seemed to be thinking. His hair was jet black. In his eyes there lurked an expression which seemed habitual to him—an expression of suffering, of sorrow subdued, smouldering but not extinguished. This expression lent a saddened aspect to his whole countenance. It did not wholly melt away even when he smiled; when in his reflective moods, it grew hardened into bitterness, to what, to a stranger, might have seemed an expression full of malignancy.

He had a low rich voice, and as he continued reading the spirit of the sacred volume seemed to infuse its pathos into his tones, subduing them to softness, almost to music.

He sat thus for a quarter of an hour, then closing the book he looked up. The sick man lay with his eyes closed, evidently in a slumber. Being unwilling to disturb him, Belmont laid the book upon a table, and softly left the cabin.

The next day the surgeon told him that the young man had requested to see him again. "I must retail you his compliment," continued the surgeon : "he whispered to me that you had one of the sweetest voices he had ever heard. It seemed to soothe him, he said, and he asked me to request you to visit him whenever you felt disposed or at liberty."

Belmont smiled gravely. "Though a deserved, his is a hard fate," he said.

"I suppose you didn't begin to cross-examine him?"

"No; nor do I think I shall. It is no business of mine, Mr. Wilkins."

"You will pardon me, Mr. Belmont, but I think it is; and I will tell you why. You yourself have some valuable cargo on board, have you not?"

"About three thousand five hundred pounds: no more."

"Well, sir, quite enough to make you regret its loss. It was evidently the intention of these men to sink the ship. Of that there can be no doubt. Everything favoured their design. We were close to land, and all hands could easily have been saved by the boats. Upon this they must have speculated. The vessel would have been found in a sinking state before the morning, and we should have had time to save ourselves. Now, sir, one cannot but presume that these men must have had some object other than enmity to the captain or shipowners, to scuttle the vessel. It is a fearful crime which might have cost us our lives, and we are bound if possible to discover its motive. The captain and myself have hitherto failed to elicit even a word upon the subject from the prisoner. We therefore look to you as our last hope. If you have not succeeded before a week's time, the sea will hide the secret as well as the body of the man for ever."

Belmont listened to this speech in silence; at last he said: "Well, I will do my best. I will not promise success: but I will try to ensure it." Then he went to the side of the ship and assumed his favourite position: leaning his shoulder against the rigging, folding his arms upon his breast, and standing thus motionless looking into the water.

For three days successively Belmont visited the sick man; sometimes holding a short conversation with him, though never touching upon the subject of the crime. He sometimes stayed with him two hours at a time, the greater part being occupied in the perusal aloud of the Bible.

On the fourth day, when he entered the cabin, he found the prisoner sitting up in his cot, his back supported by a pillow placed on the top of a pile of coats. He was engaged in reading a paper, which, on the entrance of Belmont, he hastily folded up and concealed beneath the bed-clothes.

Belmont remarked this at a glance, but he made no remark. He addressed a few words, as usual, to the man, expressive of hopes of his recovery, and then drawing a chair to his side, seated himself.

"I am glad to see you sitting up, Johnson; this augurs well for the future," said Belmont.

The prisoner shook his head with a languid smile; then suddenly opening the front of his shirt, he pointed to his breast. "You can see nothing here," he said, "but if you were to remove the skin, you would find beneath frag-ments of crushed bones, of torn muscles, and bloodless vessels. Oh, the pain, the pain I have suffered!"

"Poor fellow!" sighed Belmont. "You must, indeed, have suffered!"

"Ay, God alone knows how badly! But it's very kind of you, sir, to take the trouble to come and sit, and talk, and read with me like this. I don't deserve it from you—least, perhaps, of any on board."

"You have meditated, and nearly executed, a terrible crime, Johnson," said Belmont, in a low voice; "but it would be cruel to upbraid you with it now. Let us hope that God will permit your sufferings here on earth to expiate your sin. He is merciful and good. He may forgive you afterwards."

"Do you think He will?" asked the man, eagerly.

"I believe He will," answered Belmont, devoutly. "Though morally your crime loses nothing of its atrociousness because it was not completed, still I believe your penitence may avail, and secure your forgiveness from One who permits villains, oh, how far greater than thou, to walk this earth in peace and security." His voice sunk as he concluded this speech, and his head slightly bowed itself upon his breast.

"Mr. Belmont," said the sick man, "I was aware that you had some cargo aboard of the ship, but then I didn't know you as I know you now. Had I done so," he added, solemnly, "I swear, before heaven, I shouldn't have attempted what I did."

"Had the captain offended you, that you sought this mode of revenging yourself?"

The sick man did not seem to pay any attention to this remark: but continued, still with a
certain solemnity in his manner, "I had no intention to cause any murder by drowning. I
swear it! I wanted only to sink the ship. I
wouldn't have harmed a single hair on the head of
any one of the crew. I knew they would all
escape—for there was land on each side of us,
and the boats were all ready for lowering."

"So," thought Belmont, "the surgeon's conjecture was right."

"Will you tell the men this?" continued the
man; "they think I wanted to drown them; but
it is false! I swear by the heaven, into which I
may not be permitted to enter, that it is false! I
only wanted to sink the ship—oh, fool, fool
that I was to try it! what has it brought me
to?"

"Do not think me," said Belmont, in a quiet
voice, "impertinently inquisitive if I ask you a
question. I know you have refused to answer
the inquiries of the captain and surgeon. Therefore I cannot hope that you will treat me with
more favour. But look," he said, rising, seizing
the man's hand, and speaking in an impressive
manner, "whether you are destined sooner or

later to leave this world, it is more than useless now to conceal your secret from those so anxious to discover it. What that secret is, you alone can say. Before you attempted this crime, you must have been incited to it by promises of some kind. You could not have undertaken it on your own determination, for you could not possibly have had any object in doing so. Who this person or these persons were that seduced you into this act you alone can tell; if, on the contrary, you alone are responsible for what you attempted, then why conceal your motives? See what this act has brought you to! Cut off in the prime of life, almost broken-hearted upon a bed of such agony as you have declared no one on earth can know besides yourself; if restored to health, doomed when on shore to expiate your crime by a long and cruel imprisonment, and if fated to perish, to be consigned to the ocean with a stranger's tear alone to deplore you, and with an angry body of men to execrate your memory—such are the fruits of your attempt! if incited by others behind you, such are the results of their incitement! Terrible results indeed! Would they had not been so! What—what is your secret?"

He spoke with passionate energy : he grasped the hand of the man with an imploring gesture ; and his heart oppressed with the scene of suffering he had himself described, and of which the reality was before him, infused into his voice a pathos that lent an eloquence to his appeal such as all words would have failed to impart.

The man bowed his head upon his breast, and there came a long silence. He seemed to be wrapped in thought : his right hand was beneath the bedclothes grasping something which he appeared to be turning round and round with his fingers, and his lips were moving, though there was no articulation audible. Belmont still retained his left hand, and was gazing earnestly upon his face.

At last the man raised his head and fixed his eyes upon Belmont's. He made one or two efforts to speak : twice he failed ; at last came the words, uttered in a hoarse whisper, " I will tell you all."

Belmont let fall his hand, and bent his head down in a listening attitude.

The sick man waved his hand with a deprecating gesture, and said, " No, no, pen and ink."

Belmont instantly left the cabin, and presently

returned with his writing-desk. This he opened, and extracting from it a sheet of paper, prepared himself to listen and to write.

"Why should I not tell you?" said the man, apparently more to himself than to Belmont. "You have been kind to me: you have pitied me—pitied me! Ah! I need pity—and for why? he drove me to it—five hundred pounds—it was a tempting offer—for what? for this—for death!"

He stopped short, and then putting his hand under the bedclothes, he produced a paper, which he read through to himself, lying back against the pillow, his face pale, and his lips moving. Belmont remained silent, biting the end of his pen, and watching him.

"Is the door locked?" asked the sick man, suddenly.

"No."

"Will you lock it, please?"

Belmont rose up and did so; after which he resumed his position before his desk.

"Once more I must trouble you. Will you prop my head up higher yet. I can talk better so. Thank you." Then, after a pause, he exclaimed, "On oath! Write that."

Belmont wrote it.

"Now write as I speak. I, James Johnson, second mate of the ship 'Water Witch,' do swear and solemnly affirm, on the oath of a dying man, that what herein is stated is true."

He consulted the paper he held in his hand, and then, in a low voice, he continued :—

" On the first of September, in the year 1851, I received a letter from a firm signing itself Spenser, Murray, and Co., shipbrokers, requesting my attendance on the following morning at eleven o'clock. I went, and was shown into an office where was seated a man, who bowed to me, and then got up and shut the door. ' I must introduce myself to you as Mr. William Murray,' said he, ' and——' " The sick man suddenly paused, observing the countenance of Belmont with amazement. The pen had fallen from his hand; his eyes were dilated with a look of doubt, of horror, of incredulity ; his forehead was bedewed with beads of perspiration that had suddenly burst forth from his skin; and his whole appearance seemed as if he had been electrified. With a cry he sprung to his feet, and grasped the sick man's arm. " Tell me," he cried, trembling violently, and speaking so hurriedly that his listener followed with difficulty his meaning, "was this man thin and dark, with a black moustache and bent shoulders?"

"That's the man," was the reply.

"Had he a sly manner of looking at you from the corner of his eyes?" continued Belmont; "a strange mark upon his forehead like a crease, on a line with his nose, which gave him, even when he smiled, a bad and ominous look?"

"Why, you know him!" exclaimed Johnson.

"Know him!" A dark look swept across the features of Belmont, and he concealed his face in his hands. Then, looking up, he exclaimed, "Listen! This man has committed three murders! As a treble murderer I know him. Do not look surprised; I will tell you his victims: my wife, myself, and now, you!"

Johnson eyed him with amazement; but Belmont had taken his seat again at his desk, and was preparing to write. "Speak," he said, "what you have to tell me first; I will interrupt you no more. We can converse afterwards."

But the sick man's thoughts had been dissipated by his surprise; and in order to recover them he had first of all to consult his paper, after a while he recommenced, and went. on thus :—

"He introduced himself to me as Mr. William Murray, and appeared very polite in his manner, asking me if I would have a glass of wine, and so forth. After looking at him attentively, I remembered having once or twice seen him come on board this ship in the London Docks, when I was serving as third mate. I will not bother you with telling all that occurred before he broached the subject in hand; how artfully he sounded me, ascertaining whether I was rich or poor, married or single, ambitious or content; trying to fathom my character, all the while amusing me by putting questions about this vessel, to which I was then appointed second mate; asking her age, her capabilities of sailing, and so on. After awhile he told me that he had purchased a fourth share in the ' Water Witch,' and that this he had insured in several different offices in various amounts, the whole forming a sum of thirteen thousand pounds, which, he said, was exactly six thousand seven hundred pounds more than the share was worth."

"Can you remember the names of the insurance offices ?" interrupted Belmont.

The man said he recollected three of them, which he detailed. Belmont carefully noted them down.

"He entered into a heap of particulars concerning the state of his means; told me that he was a poor man; and that he must have money. Then he asked me if I would like to make five hundred pounds. I was not startled at the question, for by his manner and his conversation I expected some strange proposition was about to be made to me. So I answered yes. This seemed to please him, for he went to a desk, and, extracting from it a cheque-book, wrote out an order for one hundred pounds, which he handed me. 'This,' said he, 'is in part payment of the five hundred: when you return to England you shall have the rest. And now,' said he, 'I will tell you what I expect you to do for this. You are going out in a responsible position on board the 'Water Witch;' you will therefore have many opportunities of doing what I request. In a word, I want you to scuttle her!' He spoke so coolly, that my amazement was divided between the villany of his proposition and his way of putting it. I asked him if he took me for a madman. He laughed, and said no, otherwise

he would not have summoned me to such a
conference. 'There is no chance of discovery,'
he said; 'and as for murder, your own good
sense will see that no lives are lost. You have
nothing to lose, and all to gain. You can take
an opportunity of driving a hole through the ship
in the China seas. There are numerous islands
about, and nothing is easier than for the crew to
take to the boats, and make their way to the
nearest shore. And who'll find you out?
They'll conclude that she has struck against a
reef, and by the time they are anxious to find out
the nature of the damage, it will be too late.'

"Mr. Belmont," continued Johnson, slowly
and mournfully, to his companion, who had been
and was still hastily taking down every word that
fell from his lips, "I swear to you that before I
entered that man's presence I was as innocent of
maturing or conceiving such a scheme as an
infant. I cannot, will not say, that my previous
life had been one of honesty or good conduct,—
far, far otherwise indeed. And perhaps it was
through his finding this out, that that devil hit
upon me as a fit instrument for his purpose, and
brought me near him that he might tempt me
with his money. I will not weary you with what

I said when this suggestion was first made to me. I opposed it for a long while—honestly opposed it: but he triumphed at last. He pointed out what a sum five hundred pounds would be in my pocket; what it would do for me; what pleasures it would procure; how far it would go to help me on to promotion; and so cheaply earned! the mere effort of piercing a ship's bottom, and leaving the rest to fate!

"He triumphed at last. With a greater flow of language than mine he stifled my irresolution, argued against my conscience, and in time brought me round to his own views. But before I promised to execute his wishes, I made him give me a written promise, signed by himself, in which he agreed to hand me over four hundred pounds in consideration of my sinking the ship 'Water Witch.' You may believe he hesitated a long time over this. Indeed, he first of all flatly refused; calling me an idiot for thinking him capable of putting his name to a paper, the discovery of which might hang him. I shrugged up my shoulders, and assured him that his mere verbal promise of payment was not sufficient for me. He declared he had not the money, otherwise he would pay me the whole sum. I knew this to be a falsehood; or even if it were not so he could easily have got credit. But then I saw something more in such a document as I demanded than the promise of payment. I knew that with it he would be completely in my hands, to be frightened into the payment of whatever I chose to extort. Whether he saw this or not I cannot say. He still continued to refuse, and, handing him back his cheque, I rose to leave. He called me back, and said if I liked he would try and scrape the four hundred pounds together for me before I sailed. I said that was foolish, as what guarantee then would he have that I would perform his bidding. I said 'Give me that bond: it will keep both of us in subjection. I will give you another, promising that in consideration, &c., I would scuttle the ship. We shall then be equal: if I fail, you will be able to swear against me; if you fail, I can do the same to you.' I can't remember exactly the words I used, but I know that instead of he ordering me, I came at last to order him. Man of business as he was, devil as he was in his language, I triumphed over him at last, and this was the result."

He produced the paper that he had been reading at the entrance of Belmont, and handed it to him. Then he sunk back, exhausted with the fatigue of speaking. By the time Belmont had finished the perusal of the paper, he was ready to continue.

" May I keep this ? " asked Belmont.

Johnson nodded, and then after a pause he said, " I've got very little more to say. When I first started I had determined to do the job by myself. But once conversing with the ship's carpenter, I found out that he owed a grudge to the other owners in the vessel, for having stopped his pay for something or other—I forget what. He was a savage-looking, bad man, and just the one I thought to assist me in my enterprise. I cautiously beat about the bush for a little, but finding him to be what I suspected, I plumply told him my meaning, offering him twenty pounds to assist me. He jumped at the offer at once. I felt that I had secured now an invaluable assistant: the one best fitted to accomplish an undertaking, peculiarly adapted to his craft. What more shall I say ? " He was breathing in short gasps now, and appeared terribly distressed. Belmont besought him to compose himself, and wait a little.

" I'll finish it at once.   There was no chance
of our finding an opportunity during the voyage
out, so we made up our minds to wait until we
had left Hong Kong.   The carpenter seemed to
have expected a calm off Java, for he told me so
some days before, adding that that would be the
safest and best spot to sink the ship.   He had
travelled a great deal in the China Seas, and this
may account for the truth of his prediction.
Every arrangement was made ; I saw that the
boats were ready for instant lowering, and—and
—you know the rest."

He had sunk once more back upon his pillow,
pale and trembling.   Belmont sprung forward,
fearful that he was dying.   " Sign ! sign ! " he
cried, " quick ! "   He put the pen into the quivering fingers of the man, who, after much difficulty,
succeeded in attaching to his confession a tremblingly written signature.

A thrill of exultation passed through Belmont's
frame, as he folded the paper carefully up, and
placed it in his pocket along with the other that
had been given him.   He said to the man, " Do
not let a word of what you have told me escape
your lips.   If vengeance has prompted you to
this confession—vengeance upon the man who

has brought you to this—fear not. I will revenge you amply, for your revenge will be mine."

The man bowed his head, and then in a low rattling whisper, cried, " Water, water ! "

Belmont was alarmed by the sudden alteration that had taken place in the man's features. From a deathly paleness his cheeks were rapidly growing a whitey-blue—the colour of the dead. His eyes seemed lustreless, and his lower jaw appeared gradually drooping.

Belmont darted out of the cabin, taking his desk with him, and in a few minutes returned with the surgeon. No sooner did Wilkins set his eyes upon his patient, than he exclaimed aside to Belmont, " It will be over with him in half an hour. Sooner than I expected."

" Water," whispered the dying man.

They brought him what he wanted, and he drank it with avidity. It restored him for a moment, for he raised his eyes and smiled sadly at Belmont; then they, closed again; his head drooped back, and in a few minutes he expired.

The doctor's half hour was a short one.

" Did he confess ? " asked the doctor.

" Yes," said Belmont.

" Wonderful! what was it?" cried the doctor, eagerly bending forward.

" That he had suffered three weeks' hideous agony," answered Belmont, coolly.

"Poh," said the doctor.   " How disappointing, to be sure."

CHAPTER III.

THE CONVICT.

OF the many privileges claimed by the novelist, one peculiarly his own is the freedom with which he wanders about the earth, transporting his reader east or west, north or south, as his fancy prompts him or his fiction compels. I think it right that *my* reader should be reminded of this fact, otherwise he may be tempted to apply a harder name than extravagance to my imagination, when he discovers that I am about to carry him from the very heart of the China Seas to the quiet banks of the river Thames. If, however, he will honour me with his attention, I have no doubt that before this story is concluded, my motive will be sufficiently evident.

Standing some three or four miles away from Henley, may be seen, situated upon a pleasant eminence overlooking the Thames, a little venerable church, with its belfry concealed beneath a rich growth of ivy, and its walls grey and rugged from the contact of Time. Here, of a Sunday, are wont to assemble the inhabitants of the many little cots and houses that dot the green fields in the vicinity of the Thames; and here also are wont to come 'small parties of metropolitan excursionists, to forget in the contemplation of this ancient pile and the graves that surround it, the distracting cares of commercial life and London society.

One evening a man came slowly walking along the road to Henley, and striking off into a narrow path, skirting a meadow, made his way towards the little church on the brow of the hill. Often, as he advanced, he would pause and look around him, drinking in, as it were, the beauties of the surrounding landscape, then resuming his path with a heavy sigh, as if the charms that a moment before had delighted now grieved him. An air of melancholy accompanied his movement, and his head was sometimes bowed upon his breast as if absorbed in reverie.

Having scaled the short but rather steep incline leading to the back of the church, he paused and glanced in an irresolute manner before him; then, as if mastering an overpowering emotion that had suddenly taken possession of his breast, he passed through a little wicket, and in a moment found himself alone in the churchyard.

Advancing tenderly, so as to avoid treading upon the numerous little hillocks, each with a plain piece of white wood at its head painted with a name, that obstructed the way, he passed out of this—the part of the burial-ground devoted to paupers—into a region that told of comparative wealth. After narrowly inspecting the inscriptions upon the tombstones around him, he stood at length before one upon which was written this inscription :—

SACRED
To the Memory of
EVELEEN MARION HAMILTON,
WHO DIED JUNE 2ND, 183-,
Aged 20.

Thou who by musing melancholy led,
   With pensive eye shall view these simple lines,
Know that of all these mansions of the dead,
   This grave the saddest, bitterest past enshrines.
For slumbering here lies one who found a foe
   In Life : a foe from whom Death gave release :
Life held the cup and bade her drink its woe,
   Death dash'd it down and pitying gave her peace.
Oh Death ! mysterious friend to hearts whose gloom,
   Whose pangs in thee find light, in thee relief :
Spread, mighty Death, thy shadow o'er this tomb,
   To guard its relics from a slumbering grief !

So, awed by thee, no heartless tongue in scorn
　Shall dare recall the past with impious jeer ;
But Pity's self, with tears, alone shall mourn
　The WIFE, the MOTHER, that lies buried here !

He stood for a moment before it, reading these lines; then, throwing his arms to heaven with an appealing, heart-rending gesture, his head drooped upon his breast, and the man wept.

It was a still evening; the sky was darkening to the departure of the sun that had sunk behind some blue hills in the distance, and the only sounds were the notes of a bird piping its evening lay from the dark ivy that overshadowed the belfry—notes making music of the silence.

The man remained not long standing, but, slowly sinking on his knees beside the grave, he looked up to heaven, and bowing himself until his forehead touched the raised turf, he remained motionless in prayer.

For one whole hour he moved not from this position. When he rose the night had gathered round him, and the sky was brilliant with stars. He stood wrapt in contemplation still, with his eyes fixed on the grave, and his arms outstretched as if appealing to its slumbering inmate. His lips moved, but inarticulately.

There was something gloomy, grand, sublime in the spectacle of this man, his noble figure bowed in an attitude of suffering—alone with the night, with the stars, with death.

Once he flung his hand up as if in despair. Then drawing his cloak around him, he left the churchyard, and with rapid steps took the road to Henley.

On reaching the main street, he stood for a moment beneath an oil-lamp, and referred to a slip of paper which bore upon it an address. Then resuming his way, he turned sharply down a side street, and stopped before a little house, upon the door of which he knocked with his stick, there being neither bell nor knocker visible.

A long time elapsed before there was any reply; at length he heard the shuffling of feet approaching the door, and shortly after it was opened by an old man with long white hair, who tremblingly inquired who that was?

"I wish to see Mr. Frederick Musgrave, sir; are you he?"

"That's my name, sir," said the old man; "but who are you?"

"My name is Belmont, Mr. Henry Belmont;

I was anxious to see you, and procured your direction after some difficulty from Jerkins——"

" The sexton? " interrupted Mr. Musgrave.

" Yes—the sexton belonging to that old church away there on the hill. Permit me to enter; I have walked far and should be glad of a seat."

Mr. Musgrave eyed him suspiciously; but seeing him resolved to enter, edged towards the wall, making room for him to pass. Then closing the door, he limped along the passage in a pair of old slippers, whose heels made a flapping noise at every step, and conducted his unwelcome guest into a little room, on the table of which stood a tallow candle emitting at once a very feeble light and a very bad smell. Belmont put his hat and stick down, and drawing a chair near the old gentleman, who had seated himself with his slippered feet in the fender, said " My visit is unceremonious; and for that I apologise. But I am a stranger here, and as I am anxious to make some inquiries before I return to London—which I do early to-morrow morning—I must beg you to excuse the lateness of my visit."

" Well, sir, what is your business? " asked Mr. Musgrave, fidgeting with his feet.

" I will be brief with you, as I perceive I am

not welcome. Did you ever know a lady residing somewhere in this neighbourhood of the name of Godstone—Miss Godstone ? "

" Perfectly well, sir."

" Can you tell me what has become of her ? "

" She is dead, sir ; dead these four years."

" Can you inform me if ever a niece—named Eveleen "—his voice faltered as he spoke the word—" came to reside with her ? "

" Yes, sir ; and she's dead, too."

" I am aware of that."

" Did you know her ? " asked the old man, his voice discovering curiosity ; it was too dark to remark the expression of his face.

" I did."

" Were you acquainted with her history ? " said Mr. Musgrave, who had now become the questioner.

" Of course you are ? " said Belmont, avoiding the question.

" Not intimately, sir : but enough to know it was very sad. She was the wife of a convict."

" Quite right," said Belmont.

" She died at her aunt's."

" Ha ! and where is her child ? "

" By the interest you take in the subject,"

said the old man, bending his shaggy brows, and striving to catch a glance at his visitor's face, " I presume you are a connexion—a relation ? "

" Yes," answered Belmont, carelessly; " but where did you say the child was ? "

" It was a son, you know," said the old man.

" Yes," said Belmont, " so the sexton told me. But where did you say he was ? "

" I didn't say anywhere, sir, for I haven't the least idea."

" Oh! but surely Miss Godstone——"

" There lay the singularity of it," interrupted the old man, who was rapidly growing garrulous ; " Miss Godstone never would say what she had done with him; and you know," said the old man, bending forward and speaking in a dribbling whisper, " that there were some odd suspicions about this child, though I won't offend your delicacy by repeating them. But her mysterious manner of dealing with the child, of course gave a colour to the suspicion, and I told her so. But she vowed she didn't care *that* for suspicion "—and the old man snapped his fingers; " ah, she was a fine woman in her day," he added, in the same dribbling whisper.

" I hadn't the pleasure of her acquaintance,"

said Belmont; "but tell me, is nothing known of this child?"

"Nothing," replied Mr. Musgrave, emphatically, "excepting what I have told you: which is that he is the son of Miss Godstone's niece, and I'm his godfather."

"You his godfather," cried Belmont, starting.

"Yes: his godfather. Frederick, sir—that's my name; and that's his—Frederick Williams, that's how he is called."

"Frederick William," muttered Belmont to himself, who had not heard the name distinctly; "Frederick William;" and with the emotion of a father he murmuringly repeated the name over and over again.

"That's his name," said Mr. Musgrave. "Have you visited the churchyard up yonder?"

"Yes."

"Did you see Eveleen's grave? That's my tombstone over her."

"Yours!"

"Yes; and my poetry: did you read it?"

"I did; I was much affected by it."

"It cost me a heap of money to erect; but I was touched by her story, and thought her worth it. I was richer then than I am now. Once upon a time I burned two candles, and they were wax: now I can only afford one, and that's tallow! heigho!" The old man sighed heavily, and looked about him with an uncertain stare.

"If it's not a rude question, what, may I ask, was the cost of her tombstone?"

"Nine pound, eleven and sixpence, "said the old man, after a moment's reflection.

"Oh!"

"Cheap, sir, too: for there's plenty of work in the poetry."

"There is."

Then came a pause, and then Belmont, rising, said, "you can give me no further information about this child, or—or—the mother?"

"No, sir, except what I have told you: that the mother died when the child was born; and after a few years the child was sent Miss God-stone alone knows where!"

"Thank you; I am extremely obliged to you for your information. And now, sir, I hope you will not be offended at what I am going to say to you," said Belmont, drawing his pocket-book out, and opening it: the old man's eyes glistened, and he rose from his chair. "The truth is, I cannot permit you to bear the expenses of that tombstone erected to my—to—to—" he paused, and then said :, " besides, the poetry is valuable and worth much—at least, to me. You will therefore allow me to hand you this cheque—nay—" as the old man made a show of refusing—" take it—not from Belmont the stranger—but from me, Hamilton, the husband of Eveleen, who claims a husband's right to repay the cost of a wife's tombstone."

He held out the cheque : it was for one hundred pounds ; but the old man neither saw it nor accepted. He stood transfixed, his hands outspread, and his eyes dilated and staring. All at once he uttered a cry :—" Hamilton—Hamilton ! the convict Hamilton in my house !—a convict—offering me—money ! oh, go away—go away ! the cheque may be forged—you would implicate me in a crime !—go away ! I am an old, old man—I am honest, sir—honest ! oh, go ! go !"

His excitement seemed so great that he actually advanced towards his visitor and pushed him in the direction of the door; then reeling, he spun round, and fell backwards into his armchair, waving his hands and feebly crying " go—go ! I am honest—go !"

A terrible look of despair overspread the

features of Belmont, and he turned deadly pale.
The agonised expression of his face was appalling, and he pressed his hands tightly across
his heart as if to prevent it from breaking. But
the emotion was only momentary. In silence he
raised his hat and stick, and moved towards the
door; but before departing he turned to look at
the old man.

He was still waving his hands and speaking,
but inarticulately. Seeing Belmont pause, he
grew again alarmed, and cried, "Go! go!"

Belmont closed the door and went out into the
street. Thrusting the cheque he still held in his
hand into his pocket he stopped and looked up.
As he did so a meteor flashed suddenly across
the sky and disappeared. He raised his hand in
the direction where it had vanished, and muttered
through his clenched teeth, "I will be as that
light. The Hamilton that was shall be no more.
I will tear out my heart and bury it in the grave
of my Eveleen! There shall be no more love,
pity, gladness, with me or for me! So I swear
by the sacred spirit of my dead wife who stands
beside me now, and weeps!"

CHAPTER IV.

OLD ACQUAINTANCE.

On reaching London the next day, Belmont went to a hotel in Piccadilly, and having bespoken there a dinner and a bed, sallied forth into the street. He walked along leisurely, glancing at the shops as he passed, until he came opposite one over which was written, " T. Turcq, Wig-maker, &c." Having entered, he was bowed upstairs by a civil little man in a white apron, who asked him for his orders.

" Shave me," said Belmont.

" Clean, sir ? " said the hairdresser.

" No, my whiskers only; leave my moustache."

When this operation was performed, Belmont said,—

" Now I want my moustache dyed."

" What colour, sir ? "

" One that will assimilate with grey hair."

The man eyed him with curiosity, then came to the conclusion that he was a nobleman bent upon some freak. He commenced scratching his head, and presently said,—

"I don't know what to recommend, sir; grey's a difficult colour to match, and one can't dye grey."

"Haven't you a liquid that will streak my moustache with white, so as to give it the appearance of turning grey?"

The man went to a drawer, and produced a bottle.

"Are you in a hurry, sir?"

"Not for half an hour or so."

"That will do, sir. It strikes me this stuff will produce just the effect you want."

He took a small brush and carefully streaked down Belmont's moustache here and there with it.

"In ten minutes time we shall be able to see, sir. It's a stuff of my own make. I have sometimes applied it successfully; but it don't take on all hair alike."

Belmont eyed his moustache impatiently in the mirror. After waiting seven or eight minutes he perceived the parts touched by the brush to be growing a lightish red, then a pale yellow, and presently they turned white—the silvery white of old age.

"Superb!" he cried. "Give me a bottle of that stuff."

"It's very expensive, sir," said the man.

"How much?"

"I can't let you have it under four guineas. I hardly make five shillings by it even at that price."

Belmont threw down the money, and put the bottle in his pocket.

"It will last you for ten years, sir," said the man.

"Very well." Before leaving he took another glance at himself in the glass. The metamorphosis was singular and complete.

"I don't think you'll be recognised now, sir," said the hairdresser, brushing his coat; "you'll be taken for a furriner."

"Do I look like one?"

"The living image, sir."

And the hairdresser spoke the truth. When Belmont returned to his hotel, he asked the waiter if his dinner were ready.

"May I ask your name, sir?"

"Belmont."

The man looked at him incredulously.

"You wasn't the gent as came here this morning, sir, was you?"

"Of course I am! Why, my good fellow, what has become of your memory?"

"The gentleman as came here this morning, sir," said the waiter, "callin' himself Mr. Belmont, warn't no more like you than I am, sir. Why, sir," said the waiter, with energy, "he was the exact reverse!"

"You are dreaming!" said Belmont, feigning anger, but secretly delighted at the success of his alterations. "Come, get me my dinner. My name is Belmont; I came here this morning, and if you will go up to No. 26 room, you will find my portmanteau there." And pushing by the bewildered waiter—who, on hearing the number of the room, felt that there could be no longer any doubt upon the subject—he entered the dining-room, and seated himself at the table. One person occupied the apartment besides himself; this was a young man, who, shortly after Belmont's entrance, rose and went out.

"There's only one gent in the smoking-room, sir," said the waiter to him when he had con-

cluded his meal, " if you'd like to smoke a cigar,
sir."

" Have you a London Directory?" asked
Belmont.

" Yes, sir ; but if you're a-goin' to the smokin'-
room, you'll find one on the table."

" That'll do," said Belmont, and drawing out
his cigar-case, he repaired to the apartment indicated to him by the waiter.

He found the Directory, which he hastily
turned over until he came to the letter S. Then
running his finger down the column, it stopped at
these names : " Spenser, Murray, and Co., Shipbrokers, Little Tower Street, City." Having
copied this address into his pocket-book, he
glanced up and perceived the young man, whom
he had noticed in the dining-room, lounging upon
a sofa and smoking a cigar.

He was a handsome young fellow, rather short,
but with an intelligent blue eye and a fair moustache. A certain soldier-like demeanour about
him hinted to Belmont that he might be a military
man, and after a little conversation he found this
to be the case.

"Yes," said the young man, in a slightly affected
tone, " I'm home on sick leave after two years at

Bombay, where I have left 'my regiment. Do you know Bombay?"

" I do not."

" It's a sickly hole. Travelling they say enlarges the mind, but as far as my experience goes I find that travelling enlarges nothing but the liver." He laughed languidly at his joke, and then asked Belmont if he had travelled.

" Slightly."

" Ah; perhaps you know the Continent?"

" No, I do not."

" Perhaps, then, your knowledge of the world is limited to England?"

Belmont eyed him with a smile, and then changed the topic by asking when he proposed joining his regiment?"

" Oh, heaven knows!" said the young man. "I don't think I shall go out again. I detest the life, and shall cut it."

" Ah! you are lucky if you can."

" Why?"

" Because it proves you to be a man of means."

" Quite the contrary, I assure you," said the young man. "I cut it, not only because I dislike it, but because I am deucedly hard up."

"Ah!" said Belmont, "I am sorry to hear it. Poverty is a bad companion in this world."

"Well, you may call it poverty if you like, though it isn't exactly that; but even if it were, I shouldn't be ashamed of it. I'm never ashamed of what I cannot help. No man should be! When the heart acquits the man of what the world may call a wrong, it is a poor pride that blushes at it."

He spoke with warmth, and Belmont, gratified at so sensible a speech from one whom he had first of all felt inclined to consider a fop, drew his chair nearer to him and held out his cigar-case. The young man accepted a cigar in silence, and proceeded to light it.

"You will I am sure pardon me my curiosity," said Belmont, "if I ask you what you purpose doing when you leave the army?"

"Certainly. I think I shall try my fortune out in Australia."

"One of the finest fields in the world for industry; but then the industry must be unflagging."

"So it must be everywhere to win success."

"That is true."

"Do you know Australia?"

"Very well."

"Ah, I had a design many years ago of trying my luck there. I don't know what stayed me. I was the son of an officer, and my mother, who was a widow, desired to see me pursue my father's profession. She was a poor woman, and had to stint herself to purchase me a commission. How she did it, I can't tell you; but she did. I was a banker's clerk before I entered the army."

"Were you indeed?"

"Yes; I was nine months in the city, in a bank called the 'United British Banking Company.'"

Belmont started; and then in a low voice exclaimed: "How singular!"

"Why?"

"Nothing—nothing; only many years ago I knew a young fellow in the same bank; a manager of one of its branches."

"What was his name?"

"Hamilton."

"Oh, I remember; the fellow who was transported for forgery?"

"The same."

"I didn't know him; but I recollect reading an

account of it in the papers. It made a great impression upon me at the time, for—for——"

" Why ? "

" Because it might have been my fate once ! " the young man answered, mournfully.

Belmont looked at him earnestly, and then said—

" Tell me how."

" I don't suppose I should have remembered it," continued the young man, " had it not been for one name which occurred in the evidence against the prisoner."

" Which was ——? "

" Sloman."

" You knew him ? "

The young man nodded with an angry gesture.

" He was a fellow clerk of yours, perhaps ? "

" He was. The moment I perceived his name amongst the witnesses, a strange idea took possession of me that young Hamilton was innocent."

" That was curious."

" I will tell you why. It is a strange story ; but strange as it is, it nearly broke my heart at the time. This fellow, Sloman, I must tell you, was in the bank at the same time that I was.

I remember him perfectly well. He was an ugly
brute, half a Jew, with wiry locks and a hooked
nose. One day, I remember, he called me a hard
name, because I had taken his pen by accident
from his desk, and, very indignant, I retorted by
calling him a Jew. He looked at me for a
moment with flashing eyes, but made no remark
at the time. The next day something brought
him to my desk—I forget what it was, but, I
fancy, to refer to a ledger I used to keep. He
approached me quite close, and stood a longer
time by my side than I thought was necessary.
I took no notice of it, but felt very glad when
he had removed his humpbacked shape away
from me. That evening a twenty-pound note was
found missing from the chief cashier's till. None
of us were allowed to leave until the error was
detected, and I remember there was a great fuss
about it amongst the clerks at the time; every one
looking with suspicion at every one else. A
quarter of an hour passed, during which time
there was nothing heard but a hum of voices
reckoning up the figures of the day's work. My
position was at the furthest end of the bank, and
I remember I was talking with a lad about my
own age, when suddenly I heard my name shouted

out, and, looking round, perceived 'the manager, Mr. Swallow, beckoning to me. Perfectly unconscious of what he wanted, I went towards him, and as I did so, Sloman came out of the back room and took his seat at his desk. I was too much flurried to notice this at the time, but afterwards remembered it. The manager called me into his room, and in a stern voice said, ' Mr. Collins, I am given to understand—never mind by whom or how—that you know something of this missing note. You will please allow me to search you.' You may imagine my feelings ! Indignantly I demanded his authority for such a suspicion, but, without answer, he approached and commenced searching me. I was young, and knew that any opposition would result in my own discomfiture. He felt in all my pockets, and at last came to the left-hand pocket of my waistcoat. He put his fingers down in it, and extracted all that it contained. I looked at his hand, and perceived he held my keys, a slate pencil, some shillings, and a piece of paper. He opened this last, and it proved to be the twenty-pound note ! "

The young man paused and wiped his forehead. Belmont's eyes were fixed upon him with a gaze of eager anxiety.

"I will not," he continued, after a short time, "attempt to express to you the state of my feelings at that moment. Even at this distance of time, I cannot recall them without a shudder. I fell upon my knees—I was a mere boy then, sir, and more than that, I was innocent—I declared, with an eloquence that, from one so young, seemed to surprise even the cold-hearted manager, that I knew nothing of the matter. Mr. Swallow said nothing, but going out, dismissed the clerks, and returned to me, saying that he would not give one of my age into custody, but that I belonged no longer to the bank, and so forth. I went home to my widowed mother, and told her what had occurred. I feared that she would not believe me, but, thank God! she did. I felt comforted, and declared that while my mother and my conscience acquitted me of this crime, I cared not what the world might think."

"And whom did you suspect of this tremendous villany?"

"Sloman. Though I could not account for his motive, I instinctively felt that it was he who had secreted the money in my pocket; and afterwards I remembered that I had met him issuing from the manager's room, where, of course, he had been laying information against me."

" Every day," murmured Belmont to himself, " adds one more to the list of these two scoundrels' victims." Then aloud he said, " You are right—it was Sloman."

" How do you know ? " asked the young man, in an accent of surprise.

Belmont felt he had nearly committed himself. He slightly blushed, and then said, " Did you not yourself say so ? "

" Yes; but I could not swear to it. What could have been his motive ? "

" Revenge."

" For what ?"

" For calling him a Jew."

" It is incredible. Not the devil himself would devise such a scheme of villany for so petty a cause."

" *Comme vous voulez !* " said Belmont, rising. " Well, sir, I am delighted to make your acquaintance. I intend stopping here whilst I remain in town, and shall often hope to see you."

" You are very good," the young man answered. " I go into apartments to-morrow, and here is my card. I need hardly say how charmed

I shall be to welcome you whenever you feel disposed to call upon me."

" When do you propose leaving for Australia ? "

" My mind is made up for nothing yet. I have
only myself to consult, and that, you know, is the
hardest thing to agree with. I shall wait awhile
—perhaps something better may turn up."

" If I can find an opportunity of serving you,
you may depend upon me," said Belmont. And
courteously bowing to the young man, he left the
room. As he went upstairs he inspected the
card that had been given him ; it bore upon it
this inscription :

" MR. FRANK COLLINS."

And under it, in pencil, was scratched, " No. —,
Jermyn Street, St. James'."

" I'll make him my friend," thought Belmont ;
" perhaps he may be of service to me some day.
First Murray—then Sloman !"

He rose late the next morning, and when he
inquired after his young friend of the preceding
night, he learned that he had left an hour or so
before. Bidding the waiter secure him a cab, he
took a hasty breakfast, and jumping into the
vehicle, ordered the man to drive into the City.

He remained lost in reverie the whole distance of the drive. At last the cab stopped with a jerk, and glancing up, Belmont perceived himself to be in Little Tower Street.

" What number, sir ? " cried the cabman.

" All right; this will do." And jumping out, Belmont paid the man his fare and walked up the street, looking at the numbers of the houses as he passed. He stopped at length before an opened door, beside which was placed a plate, bearing the name of " Spenser, Murray and Co.," and, biting his lip to subdue the involuntary emotions that blanched his cheek, he entered.

" Is Mr. Murray in? " he asked of an old grey-headed clerk, who sat behind a desk with a curtain, writing.

The clerk looked up, and said, " No, sir."

" Mr. Spenser, then ? "

" There is no Mr. Spenser."

" Who can I see ? "

" Mr. Sloman is in, sir." Then suddenly raising his voice, he cried, " Mr. Sloman."

A back door opened, and the hunchback entered. A momentary sickness dimmed the eyes of Belmont, but with a vast effort he stifled the emotion, and coldly returned Sloman's bow.

The hunchback was unaltered in appearance, his face alone being more yellow, and his eyes more sharp and restless. The fifteen years that had rolled by seemed to have left him untouched.

It was a supreme moment for Belmont. Sloman's eyes were upon him, scrutinising his appearance with apparent curiosity, but not the faintest token of recognition escaped him; not by the feeblest sign did he betray his recollection of the man before him.

But there was one more ordeal for Belmont to go through. Could he hope that his voice would not be recognised by those large ears that gaped on either side of Sloman's head?

"I wish to see Mr. Murray; is he in?"

This was said in a natural tone: it was a test to the memory of the hunchback. But Sloman answered, "No, sir;" and a feeling of exultation thrilled through Belmont's heart: for he knew that if he could deceive *this* man, he could deceive the whole world.

"He won't be long, sir; meanwhile, won't you walk in and sit down?" He led the way to a back office, and offered Belmont a seat.

"I have just returned from China, and having shipped some tea in a vessel called the 'Jasper,'

I have called to give you the consignment. You were recommended to me by a house at Hong Kong."

"You are very kind, sir. We shall be most happy to execute your orders. I'll just go and hurry Mr. Murray—for I know where he is." And he left the office.

Belmont had not expected to meet this man here. He knew not, indeed, where he was; and he was going to make it his business to find him out. A feeling of delight possessed his mind to think he had found them thus together; for all at once an extraordinary thought had presented itself to his mind: a conception—a creation which he grasped with all the thirst of a deep revenge. It had been awakened in him by the presence of Mr. Sloman: it had rushed upon him in the first contact of their eyes; and now that he was left alone for these few minutes, he elaborated, with the rapidity of a brilliant imagination, a scheme such as before he could never have realised: such as before he would have given half his fortune to be enabled to pursue.

He looked carefully around him, and inspected the room in which he was seated. It was a little,

ordinary office, furnished as such offices usually
are, with a safe, a table, a few chairs, and a chest
of drawers. But what seemed to please him
most was a door which opened at the side. He
rose and looked out. He found that it connected
itself with a narrow passage that led to a private
door in the street. The passage was dark, and
on looking down it he perceived another door a
few yards away from where he stood, which he
saw opened into the office in front. All this he
noticed with a rapid eye. What there was singular about it I cannot tell; but certain it is that
the inspection seemed to satisfy him, for when he
resumed his seat he was smiling.

The revenge of such men as Belmont has a
prescience in it which, whilst it admits of no
explanation, is as unerring in its estimate of the
future, as if the results of that future were
already before it. He had laid a train in his
mind which needed but a spark to ignite it. And
evidently the room in which he was seated was to
furnish that spark. Not that I would seek to
justify his vengeful schemes by pleading the
wrongs that inspired them. But if I do not
seek to justify him, I cannot but hesitate to
condemn him. I cannot but remember that he

received at the hands of the two men, to chastise whom he was about to devote his life and his fortune, an outrage, a wrong, such as the meekest nature in the world would have risen to resent. Let us at least proportion the evil of revenge to the enormity of the provocation : and compensative as nature or fate may be in her dealings with the human mind by the operations of conscience, vengeance such as Hamilton's must lose something of its blackness when we consider that its desire to accelerate human retribution is animated by the recollection of one of the foulest, the most unprovoked of wrongs ever offered by man to man.

CHAPTER V.

A STARTLED KNAVE.

AFTER an absence of five minutes, Sloman returned.

He came in apologising for his abrupt departure, and for the absence of Mr. Murray, who he regretted to say was not likely to return under a quarter of an hour, business of a particular and urgent nature demanding his presence.

" Are you his partner ? " asked Belmont.

Sloman paused, and looked rather fidgetty, and then said, " Not exactly, sir; but he entrusts me with the management of his business in his absence."

" Oh! well, I think I'll wait for Mr. Murray, as I have other matters of a confidential nature to communicate to him, besides my own business."

Sloman looked at him sideways, and coughed.

It was one of those hollow coughs which the hearer may fill with what meaning he likes. He held a newspaper out to Belmont, who declined it, saying that he had read it at his hotel.

"Yours, I suppose," said Belmont, in a careless and conversational tone, "must be a very lucrative business?"

Sloman shrugged his shoulders, and said, "middling."

"I suppose, though, it requires years to secure a connection, and even then you cannot always depend upon it being profitable?"

"You are quite right, sir. It wants a shrewd head to get on in ship-brokering."

"I suppose you are thoroughly acquainted with it?"

"I ought to be; I've been at it now getting on for six years."

"And not in business for yourself yet!"

Sloman gave a cautious smile, and answered, "I am waiting."

"Ah, you are lucky to have the patience to wait. But that, after all, I believe, is the only way to succeed—patience, and, of course, industry."

"When do you expect the 'Jasper' in?"

asked Sloman, suddenly changing the conversation.

"Soon, I hope: say about three weeks' time."

"I know the ship well; she is a favourite in the China trade."

"I believe she is. I came home in another favourite, called 'The Water Witch;' do· you know her?"

He glanced keenly at Sloman as he spoke; there was nothing, however, in his manner to indicate that the mention of the vessel caused him any uneasiness. "*He's* not in the secret," thought Belmont.

"Oh, yes; very well," said Sloman, in reply to Belmont's former question. "I knew the second mate of her, too—Johnson. I made his acquaintance in this office."

"Ah, indeed."

"Did he return with the ship?"

"No; he died coming home."

"Why, he was a young man: what caused his death?"

"Some illness or other."

"Oh! he seemed a promising young man, too. I had a long chat with him here one morning, when he was waiting for Mr. Murray."

Belmont glanced at his watch. " Mr. Murray will soon be in now, sir," said Sloman.

" I am stopping at the —— Hotel," remarked Belmont, in a friendly manner. " I am a stranger in London, and am therefore naturally delighted to see anybody who cares to pop in upon me of an evening. Here is my card. I shall be glad of your company whenever you feel disposed to call. Stay :—will you come and smoke a cigar with me to-morrow evening? You can give me a hint upon some of the China trading ships, which will be of service to me as a merchant."

Belmont had admirably calculated upon the effect of this speech. To Sloman its abruptness was a source of additional gratification. It was vastly complimentary to begin with. Here was an utter stranger spontaneously requesting his society—requesting it after an interview of a few minutes. The vanity of this hunchback was more than a match for his cunning. Whatever his acuteness might have suspected, his vanity would have instantly dismissed. But this merely supposing that there *was* anything to suspect. On the contrary : here was a stranger cordially inviting another stranger to visit him. Who the first stranger was, it mattered little. It was ap-

parent that he was at all events respectable, and
—rich.   Take it which way you like, it was flattering—it was mighty flattering.   So thought the
hunchback : and so Belmont *knew* he would
think.

He poured forth his thanks to Belmont for his
politeness, and assured him that he would be at
the hotel on the next evening.   Would eight
o'clock do ?   It would.   At eight o'clock then,
he would be there.

At this moment Murray entered.

Time, however well it may have treated Sloman, had acted in a more unfriendly way to
Murray.   His hair and moustache were still
black, but there was a hollowness, a yellowness
about the cheek, an expression of habitual
anxiety in the mouth and eyes, a network of
wrinkles upon the forehead, an uncertain, agitated, hesitating manner about him, that told of
a worse enemy than Time—Care !   He entered
hurriedly, anxious for business : and bowed to
Belmont, who quietly returned the salute.   The
manner of the latter was reserved, but not distant.   His triumph over the lynx-eye, the razor-
like sagacity of Sloman, had given him a complete mastery over himself.   Not the least pallor

of the cheek, not the least tremor of the lip, discovered his emotion at the presence of his deadliest foe. He stood the client, the stranger, in a strange office; never did the stage boast such a piece of consummate acting!

"Mr. Sloman hastily communicated to me your business," said Murray, making a gesture for Belmont to be seated, and taking a chair himself, " and I need hardly say we shall be delighted to execute any orders you may favour us with."

Belmont returned some civil answer, and then proceeded to the business in hand. What that business was, the reader already knows. It was a consignment of some cargo to the house of Spenser, Murray, and Co.; and before the matter could be concluded, there seemed much writing to be done, and many questions to be asked and answered.

All this time Sloman formed one of the trio, sometimes writing, sometimes speaking, sometimes listening. Belmont observed that he addressed Murray in a tone rather more peremptory than is usually the case between clerks and employers; and he also noticed, but not with the least surprise, that Murray answered him in a manner subdued and deferential.

For why should he have been surprised? Did he not know,—know with such force of conviction as made him tremble lest a sudden impulse should tempt him to burst out with his knowledge—did he not know, I say, the link by which these men were connected?"

When the business was concluded, Belmont said, " Mr. Murray, I am anxious to have a five minutes' conversation with you. Will you permit me?"

" Certainly:" and then he added, seeing Belmont pause, " there are no secrets here, sir," and he glanced half shyly at Sloman.

" I should prefer ——" began Belmont.

" Mr. Sloman and I, sir, are one," interrupted Murray; " whatever is told to one is generally communicated to the other. If what you have to tell is confidential, we—that is Mr. Sloman and myself—will pledge you our word to maintain secresy."

" It is impossible; I regret that I should be the means of infringing the rules of an union which I am sure "—with a smile at Murray— " must be mutually pleasing; but what I have to say cannot be uttered in the presence of a third person. I think you will hardly require me to say more."

Murray cast an imploring look at Sloman, who slightly shrugged his shoulders, and then went towards the door leading into the front office, which he closed after him.

There came a pause, and Murray assumed the attitude of a man prepared to listen. Belmont, however, seemed in no haste to commence; his head was bent as if in thought, and he remained for some moments in this position. All at once something seemed to arouse him. He rose from his chair, and glanced cautiously around him. Then he approached the door leading into the passage, which he opened, and looked out. There was evidently something outside to amuse him, for the faintest possible smile lurked in his mouth, as he said, " You will pardon my caution ; when you have heard my communication, you will understand it."

He came and sat down opposite to Murray, leaving the door which he had opened slightly ajar. But neither of them seemed to notice this : Murray was gazing with a look of anxiety on the face of his companion.

" I suppose," began Belmont, "that your clerk told you that I had recently returned from China ?"

" No, he said nothing about it."

" Well, such is the case. Moreover, it may interest you to know that I came home in a ship called the ' Water Witch.' "

A horrible paleness overspread Murray's features, but he remained silent.

" She was a fine ship, sir ; a fast-sailing craft, the swiftest on the line, so her commander told me ; did you ever see her ? "

It was the cat playing with the mouse.

" Yes—yes, only once—it was in the London Docks."

" There was a man on board of her who served as a second mate—named Johnson, apparently a very respectable man. The captain seemed to repose great confidence in him, and during the run from Hong Kong to the islands of Java and Sumatra, he was left frequently in charge of the ship. It was by the rarest chance in the world that I detected this man to be one of the greatest scoundrels that ever walked the earth."

He paused, keenly scrutinizing the features of his companion, whose hands were convulsively grasping the sides of the arm-chair, and whose features were possessed of an expression of the most abject horror—the most abject fear.

" How I did this I will not weary you by de-
tailing, but it will surprise you to know that I
was the means of preventing him from scuttling
the ship, and sinking her with probably all hands
on board. He is dead, you know."

An expression of relief flashed across the
almost livid features of Murray, but still not a
syllable escaped him.

" Dead—but dying, I must tell you, he made a
confession that implicates you in a crime which is
considered by the law as the most serious next to
murder."

" He was a liar," half-shrieked Murray, starting up from his chair and brandishing his fist;
then falling backwards he repeated in the same
half-shrieking voice, " he was a liar—you must
not believe him, sir—on my honour—you must
not believe him."

" Patience, sir, patience," said Belmont, coolly,
" you will hear first of all what he said, before you
contradict it. To begin then, he informed me
that you—you Mr. William Murray, incited him to
this act by a promise of five hundred pounds, of
which you gave him your cheque for a hundred as
an instalment. Is this correct ? "

There was no reply, except a spasmodic shaking

of the head, and a movement of the arms, pitiably
full of supplication and fear.

" This is how he told me you were to profit
from the crime." He pulled a paper from his side
pocket, from which he read, saying, " In the first
instance you purchased a portion of the ship from
the owners, Messrs. Smythe and Lucas, for which
you paid six thousand three hundred pounds.
You then insured your shares in several offices,
amongst which were the Alliance Assurance Company, the Mutual Marine, and Lloyd's, the policies
in the aggregate amounting to the sum of thirteen
thousand pounds, being exactly six thousand
seven hundred pounds more than the share in the
vessel was worth.   Was my informant correct ? "

The agony expressed in Murray's face was terrible to witness.   In a choking voice he muttered, " a lie ! a lie ! it's all a lie ! "

Belmont shrugged his shoulders.   " A lie or
not," he said, " you see it is very perspicaciously
concocted.   But here is the man's confession,
with his name to it." He held it out, and Murray
dashing forward, grasped it with fingers that
seemed palsy-smitten, and devoured it with his
eyes.

He read it through, then shouting, " He is a

liar, and you are fool to believe him,' he tore the paper into a thousand pieces, and hurled them into the fire-place.

Belmont surveyed him with a smile. Then feeling in his pocket, he drew out two papers, one of which he held up in each hand.

" This," said he, " is the original confession— the confession of which you have destroyed the copy. *This* is *your* promissory note—with your name attached, in which you agree to pay to James Johnson, in consideration of his scuttling the ship ' Water Witch,' the sum of four hundred pounds; " and so saying he replaced the two documents in his pocket, and re-buttoned his coat.

One of those terrible looks of despair which we may imagine must overspread the face of the suicide ere he deals himself the death-blow, darkened the features of Murray. He threw his arms up to heaven, and then bursting into tears, fell prostrate at the feet of Belmont, grasping his legs and grovelling with his forehead against the floor.

" It is true, it is true," he cried, gasping in a hollow voice. " It is all true; for the love of heaven, have pity upon me. I was poor— I wanted money. Oh, mercy, mercy, do not

publicly charge me with this crime—my character, my hopes—Oh, what will become of
me?"

With folded arms and knitted brow, Belmont
surveyed the weeping, grovelling wretch beneath
him. He could have placed his foot upon his
neck, and pressed until the villain should expire!
What had he not done? Character—hopes!
What mercy had he for the character—what
mercy for the hopes of the man who proudly
stood over him, in the days gone by? Pity!
There was no longer pity on earth! It had
expired with Eveleen—why should it revive to
lament the agony of her murderer? Pity!——

He bent down and raised his foe by the arms,
and placed him in his chair. Murray dared not
look up: his face was covered with his hands,
and through his fingers rolled the molten drops
evoked from his black heart not by remorse—not
by repentance, but by the coward's fear—the coward's agony!

"Look up!" exclaimed Belmont. "You are
safe—you have nothing to fear! I will not
betray you."

He raised his eyes and encountered the noble
features of Belmont looking upon him with an

expression half of disdain, half of compassion. Ah! Nature vindicated herself in spite of him, in his heart.

"You will not betray me?—oh, swear! swear!"

"I swear."

Murray rose as if to throw his arms around his neck and embrace him. The cold eyes of Belmont repelled him, but grasping his arm, he said, in a thick, hurried voice:

"Thanks—thanks! Oh, a thousand times thanks! You have saved me from transportation, perhaps from the gallows. Oh, I thank you! And I love—ah, if *she* should know this, where would be my hopes? Yes, by your silence you preserve two—the girl of my heart and myself. Oh, you are good—good! We will be friends, sir; nay, we will be as brothers, Mr. Belmont. I could worship such a brave, generous heart as you possess! to conceal this blighting crime.... oh, you are good—good! Thanks! thanks!—a thousand times thanks." And once again he pressed forward as if to embrace him.

Belmont rose. "And now farewell, sir," he exclaimed; "you have my business, and I your secret. I will do my duty, and I expect you will do yours, in looking after my property. Farewell."

"Nay, sir, you shall not go until you promise to call upon me. I will introduce you to the girl to whom I am engaged. Then you will appreciate well your own generosity. See, here is my address." He produced a card, which he tremblingly handed to Belmont, who accepted it with a slight bow. "When will you call? Come soon—say next Wednesday. Yes; I shall expect you next Wednesday. I shall have a rubber at my house—aud my girl and her father will be there. You will be charmed with them—oh, how charmed!"

He spoke with such rapidity as to become sometimes almost incoherent. Belmont stood reflecting for a moment; presently he said:

"I will come, sir. On Wednesday next?"

"Yes, yes. Oh, how kind you are—now I shall expect you."

He paused, and then in a fawning, low voice, said:

"Won't you give me those papers?"

"No; I intend to keep them as curiosities."

"Oh, burn them."

"I promise you they shall be kept secret."

Murray gave a ghastly smile: "I will trust you—I will trust you."

"Farewell!"

"Farewell! Be secret, I implore you."

Belmont nodded and advanced towards the door leading to the passage. This he opened, and as he put his head out he perceived Sloman in the act of passing through the door into the office.

"Not that way, Mr. Belmont," cried Murray; "this door, please."

He turned back, and as he went by, Murray seized his hand with a fawning grasp, and whispered:

"Be secret—be secret! On Wednesday next, mind, at eight o'clock."

CHAPTER VI.

PUNCTUALLY at the hour he had himself named, Sloman waited upon Belmont at the hotel. He had dressed himself out a little for the occasion, not knowing but that his host might have other guests with him. His hair, which was always smooth and sleek, like his face, like his character, had an extra gloss upon it, imparted by a very large quantity of pomade, which, by causing the hair to adhere to the head, showed the contour of the skull in a way that added a good deal to the rest of his imper-fections. His face shone with the soap that he had employed to cleanse it, its yellowness contrasting forcibly with the high white shirt collar whose points mounted almost to a level with his ears. He was dressed in tight-fitting clothes: his coat, which was blue, sitting upon his back like his hair upon his head, and his trousers adhering to his legs in a way that rather too obviously demonstrated their shape and thinness. His feet were encased in a pair of low glazed shoes, fitted each with a big bow of broad ribbon.

Such was the figure whom the waiter, with imperturbable gravity, bowed to at the door; and having gathered his wants, he conducted him upstairs.

Belmont, who was seated by himself in a private apartment attached to his bedroom, rose as he entered, and shaking hands with him in the most cordial and friendly manner possible, bade him welcome, and begged him to occupy the armchair.

"I have asked no one to meet you, Mr. Sloman," he said. "Indeed, as I think I told you, my circle of acquaintances in London is very limited. However, I hope we shall be able to kill an hour or so—or more, by ourselves."

There were bottles of spirits upon the table, and cigars and tobacco. There were also implements for brewing a bowl of punch. Sloman's eyes sparkled as he perceived them, and he said :

"Aha, Mr. Belmont. I see you know how to enjoy life."

Belmont smiled, and asked him if he liked punch.

Sloman made no reply, but closing his eyes significantly laid his hands upon his stomach.

" Well, sir, pray light up and help yourself. I am an old traveller, and there is no ceremony with me. Here is brandy, whiskey, gin, and rum. Which will you have ? "

Sloman grasped the brandy bottle, and poured himself out a copious draught. Then lighting a cigar, he stretched his legs out and yielded himself up to comfort.

The conversation that ensued was trivial and common-place enough, as it mostly is for the first half-hour or so everywhere. Belmont in a short time perceived that Sloman was a drinker. No sooner did the hunchback empty his glass than he filled it again.

Sometimes Sloman would say, " You are drinking nothing yourself, sir."

" Drinking nothing ! Why, what do you call this ? " Belmont held up his glass, which was half full. " And this ? " and he held up a bottle, which was half empty.

" We'll have the punch," he exclaimed, " presently."

"Ay," said Sloman, "*Quand vous voulez.*"

You may put it down as a rule, that when an Englishman, who shuns the French language during the day, and in the absence of drink, voluntarily speaks it at night in the presence of spirits, that Englishman is in an incipient or early stage of intoxication.

That this was the case with Sloman, Belmont perceived at a glance. But though the symptoms were apparent, it was obvious that many glasses yet had to be consumed before he should be in that state of which the only happiness is incapacity of thought.

"Mr. Murray appears to be a very gentlemanly nice fellow," said Belmont. "He was recommended to me, as I told you, by some friends in China. Now, he must have earned a good business reputation to have found support in a country so distant."

"Oh, he's a shrewd fellow," said Sloman, wagging his head, and gazing at Belmont with a very watery eye.

"So I should fancy. I suppose he is the head of your firm now, since Mr. Spenser is dead?"

"Yes."

"And when do *you* propose to be at the head

of a firm, Mr. Sloman?" Belmont said, with a smile.

Sloman answed, "Before long, I suspect."

"Well, I drink to your speedy promotion!" He nodded, and put the glass to his lips.

Sloman laughed, and said, "I echo the sentiment." And he emptied his glass.

"I don't think I shall remain long in England," remarked Belmont. "We travellers cannot subsist for any length of time in one spot. You will hardly believe me, I dare say, when I tell you that though I have been in London only a few days, I am growing weary of it already."

"How long is it since you were in England?"

Belmont glanced at him carelessly, and replied, "Really, I forget how long it is. Stay!" he said, placing his hand in his pocket, and producing a pocket-book, "I can tell you to the day. I have all my memoranda here, and all my valuable papers too," he added, with a laugh, "Pocket-books are useful things, sir."

"Very," said Sloman, emptying the remains of a bottle of brandy into his tumbler.

"Now, let me see." Belmont opened the book, and, whether through design or accident, some papers fell out. He stole a swift glance at Sloman, and perceived his eyes fixed upon the papers. At the same time Sloman darted forward and picked them up.

" You have dropped these," said he. laying them upon the table.

" Thanks," said Belmont, carelessly. Then, lifting up the corner of the topmost one he peeped into it; having done which he hurriedly gathered them up, as a man would gather up anything which he did not wish to be seen, and redeposited them in his pocket-book.

Though his eyes were not raised, he knew that Sloman was watching him.

" The last time I was in England," he said, consulting his memoranda, " was in March—the third, eighteen hundred and forty-four."

" That's eight years ago," said Sloman.

" Yes; eight years ago. Ah, how the time flies! Well," he said, laying his pocket-book upon the table, and placing his hand carelessly upon it, " we have but to live our lives, and are we not right in enjoying the hours that speed so rapidly from us, as we are now doing?" And he pointed to the bottles and glasses upon the table.

" It's the only way," replied Sloman. And to

prove that it was the only way, he emptied his tumbler at a draught.

" By the bye," said Belmont, suddenly rising, and consulting his watch, " I wanted to speak to the waiter about something. Will you excuse me for five minutes ? "

" Certainly."

" Make yourself comfortable in my absence. I shan't be longer than I have said." And nodding at Sloman he left the room, closing the door tightly after him.

He went with a moderately heavy tread down as far as the first landing; but when he had reached this, he returned on tip-toe to the door, and stood with his eye fixed to the keyhole.

He could see Sloman sitting as he had left him. All at once the hunchback rose, and looked cautiously round him. He peeped into the bedroom leading out of the sitting-room, then returning, approached the door through the keyhole of which Belmont was watching him. Belmont shrunk back, fearing that he might open the door and look out; but in a moment after he heard Sloman's light, cat-like tread within, and again he resumed his post.

Sloman had gone to the table and was holding

in his hand the pocket-book which Belmont had left there—as if by chance. He was extracting the papers from it, opening them first and then replacing them. He did this very rapidly. At last he took out the two that had been dropped, and hastily peeping at them thrust them into his pocket. He placed the pocket-book as he had found it, and resuming his seat proceeded to mix himself some spirits, and smoke.

Leaving the door, Belmont noiselessly crept downstairs. At the expiration of five minutes he returned. He was profuse in his apologies to Sloman for having deserted him, and hoped that he had revenged himself by punishing the bottle.

At this moment a waiter entered bearing some hot water and a jug of milk.

"Now, Mr. Sloman, for the punch!" said Belmont. And he set about preparing it.

Evidently it was a favourite beverage of Slo- man. He drank it up with infinite relish, and was most industrious in his application of the spoon. His incipient intoxication was rapidly becoming confirmed.

"Why don't you drink, Mr. Belmont?" he cried. "Drink, sir, drink! this is rare stuff. Here!" and he raised the ladle full of the steaming liquor and extended it towards Belmont, spilling half of it over the cloth.

Belmont laughed loudly at this mishap.

"Ha! ha! I see you are a rare one, Mr. Sloman, for the 'cratur' as the Irish say. Well, commend me to the man who loves his glass."

"So say I?" cried Sloman.

> "A girl and a glass, and a pipe, by the mass!
> And a night to make love in, and drink, sirs,
> These, these are the joys of all free-hearted boys,
> As ye know——"

He paused, forgetting the rest of the words: but continued the air to its close by shouting, "Tol, lol de rol, lay! fol lol de rol, lay! oh!" wagging his head as he sung, and keeping time with his legs and arms.

"What would Mr. Murray say if he saw you?" exclaimed Belmont, glancing at him sideways and speaking with a slight laugh.

The smile on Sloman's face relaxed: he assumed an expression of sudden rage, and struck his knee heavily with his fist.

"What's Murray to me?"

"Isn't he your master?"

Sloman half bounded from his seat as he cried, "*My* master? ask him!"

"I understood him to be so."

"Murray *my* master! he knows better than to say that. A man my master whom I could hang by a word!"

All his joviality seemed suddenly to have deserted him. A vindictive scowl settled upon his forehead, and his eyes glanced fiercely at Belmont through the haze with which the fumes of the spirits had overspread them.

"You say you could hang him?" Belmont said coldly. "That is curious. Supposing Mr. Murray should say the same thing of you?"

"He wouldn't—he daren't! What's he got to say? Pish! I hate the fellow. Why don't he take me in as his partner? He promised to make me a partner—pish—but he doesn't. Who can live on four hundred a year?"

"If he promised anything to you," said Belmont, gravely, "he should fulfil that promise."

"Ay, and I'll make him! Ain't I got his secret!—in my madness I once told him I'd split—and he fell at my feet and whined—and whined—and whined" —he imitated with clasped hands, and imitated cleverly too, the accents of a supplicating man :—" ha! ha! *he* my master?"

This notion seemed to irritate him more than

all else. He continued crying in a shrill, drunken voice,

" *He* my master ? "

"If you have a secret of his, so much the better for you. Keep on threatening him with it, and you'll bring him to what you like."

" Hooray! you're the right stuff!" and Sloman got off his chair and grasped Belmont by the hand, steadying himself by clasping the edge of the table.

" That's how I like to hear a man talk. Work it into him, eh? ha! ha! you don't know what I know.

He seized Belmont's tumbler, and unconscious of what he was doing, poured its contents down his throat. Belmont's eyes were in a blaze with inward excitement: but his features remained cold and immoveable in their expression.

The liquor that Sloman had swallowed proved the maddening drop, and letting go his hold, he whirled his long arms around him, dancing about with the grotesque gesticulation of a misshapen baboon. Belmont laughed fiercely.

" Do not mind Murray!" he cried. " You are too good a man for *him*! "

" Too good! " hiccoughed Sloman, balancing

himself before his companion, "I should think so. I didn't transport a man—no, s'help me, I didn't! It was Murray—didn't he advise—ha! ha! wasn't it shrewd of him, now? He a sinner, s'help me! and all for a woman he did it—ho! ho! he's afeard of me—s'help me! look——"

His face assumed an expression of gravity hideously ludicrous: he swayed himself to and fro before Belmont, his hair over his bloodshot eyes, one hand outstretched with the finger of the other laid upon its palm. "He wanted to pay me—he was a fool—I burned his money—it was my revenge. S'help me, there!"

He laid his finger against his nose and tried to wink. Belmont rose.

"Keep your secret, and play upon Murray," he said, "as you would upon this." And he smote the table with a thundering blow. Then he sat down and watched his guest.

The hunchback was reeling about between the fireplace and the table, balancing himself against the backs of chairs or whatever he encountered. Now and then his thin legs would give way, and he sank down; but he rose again, and continued wading about here and there, talking an unintelligible jargon, and sometimes trying to sing a song.

All at once he tripped over the mat, and falling struck his forehead against a chair, and remained motionless, extended full length upon the floor.

A nasty sight, surely! Belmont rose, and turned him over with his foot; then kneeling down he felt in his pocket and drew out the papers which had been extracted from the pocket-book. He smiled as he inspected them, and putting them carefully back in the hunchback's pocket, he felt in his waistcoat and found there a card upon which was written his address. Ringing the bell, he ordered the waiter to get assistance to take the unconscious form down-stairs, put it in a cab, and have it driven to the address upon the card.

This was done, and once again Belmont found himself alone.

CHAPTER VII.

AN EVENING PARTY—WITHOUT A HOSTESS.

MURRAY had long since given up his house at Y——. He had left it the year following the death of Mr. De Courcy; and had left it cordially cursing the hour he had entered it. For, to speak truth, Murray's recollections of Y—— were neither grateful nor joyous. He had made up his mind to depart some years before he did; for the inconvenience of travelling night and morning to his business and back was far from pleasing. But all at once he was introduced to Eveleen De Courcy, and from that moment Love taught him to submit to every privation to be near the object of his affections. But, certainly, the most uncongenial memory that was attached to Y—— was to Murray his loan to Mr. De Courcy. It will be recollected that he had presented to that gentleman a blank cheque, informing him he was welcome to fill it up to any amount he liked. This Mr. De Courcy had very faithfully done; going so far as to append to this cheque a figure exceeding that of which he was immediately in want. Murray had taken no security from him; implicitly trusting to the honour of the old man. Nor is it likely that Mr. De Courcy would have given him cause to lament his trust, had not a pistol ball put a period alike to his life and to Murray's expectations of repayment. He had died intestate; and the result was the whole of the property, when Eveleen was found to be no more, went to the nearest of kin,—a remote connexion who seemed suddenly to have sprouted up in the North of England for the express purpose of securing the property. Murray of course went in with other creditors, but as he had nothing to prove his demands except his bare word, the remote connexion thought fit to repudiate his claims, and ignore with horrid coldness the whole affair.

Hence it will be seen that Murray was not unreasonable in his detestation of the town of Y——.

The loss of this money was a very serious blow to him. He had never, indeed, recovered it; and it was probably owing to this, and other matters equally unsatisfactory, that he was led into meditating the·crime of which we have already seen the result.

He had now taken a house in the neighbourhood of St. John's Wood, and here he had lived for the last five years. It was comfortable and airy, and had a garden at the back, but no more. The rooms were furnished in a manner that sufficiently attested the state of the occupant's purse. There was nothing whatever about them to show that the man was even comfortably off. The carpets were plain; the chairs, the tables, the furniture—all was plain. There were no pictures, there was not even a piano. He was a man not willing that it should be known he was not wealthy. He would talk bigly of his means, and when people said significantly, "I wonder, Mr. Murray, that you don't amuse yourself by furnishing your house superbly; it is a hobby of ours, that of luxurious appointments, and we never can understand other people not entering into our feelings. A handsomely furnished house, you know, is so delicious!" Mr. Murray would answer, "Well, I agree with you in a measure; though for my part, I love simplicity in all things: beauty unadorned, you know. Besides, to a bachelor like myself, whatever is not immediately useful is superfluous; and I must say I detest superfluity." People would then go away and call him eccentric; and he would think them impertinent. Amongst them all only one knew the truth; only one was aware that this eccentricity was nothing more than want of means. This was Murray himself.

To the house of this gentleman Belmont repaired on the night following the little scene detailed in the last chapter, and was shown up into a drawing-room prepared for the reception of guests. At one corner of the apartment stood a piano opened, with music before it. But this was not Murray's property; it had been hired for the occasion.

The entrance of Belmont seemed to cause some little excitement amongst a sprinkling of ladies who were dotted about the room, but who, as Murray darted forward to welcome him, got together in a group and spoke in whispers.

Certainly it was not often these ladies' luck to see a handsomer or nobler-looking man.

"I am so enchanted to see you!" exclaimed Murray, slightly colouring as he met the eyes of Belmont; "now, do let me introduce you at once to Mr. and Miss Lloyd." Then in a whisper he said, "she is the young lady I spoke to you about; you remember—my future bride."

"Oh, indeed!" He bowed courteously to some old gentleman in a velvet waistcoat and gilt buttons to whom Murray had led him, and afterwards to a young lady who was seated by the old gentleman's side. Belmont fixed upon her a look of curiosity; he was perhaps eager to inspect this successor of Eveleen.

She was a pretty girl, with dark eyes and black hair, and cheeks heightened with much colour. She had a charming figure, and when she smiled disclosed a ravishing set of teeth. She seemed not more than eighteen; but the moment Belmont caught her eye, a certain twinkle at the extreme corner of it told him plainly that she was not wholly ignorant of life.

"Mr. Belmont has recently returned from China," said Murray; "and as I know, Mr. Lloyd, you have a great longing to know all about the Celestial Empire, I cannot leave you in better hands." Then offering his arm to the lady he said, "Miss Lloyd, the ladies are dying to have a song from you. Let us leave these two gentlemen together, to discuss the antipodes, whilst we——"

"I really cannot sing just at present; I will later," exclaimed the young lady, interrupting a speech that was probably growing poetical.

"Nonsense! nonsense!" exclaimed the old gentleman testily, anxious for his daughter to move, that Belmont might get a seat next him. "Go and do as you're asked, Alice. What a fuss these women make about nothing, to be sure!"

Alice, thus reprimanded, rose and rather sulkily took her lover's proferred arm, who whispered something sweet in her ear to soothe her. Before she got near to the piano, however, she suddenly darted off at an angle, dragging Murray helplessly after her, and walked towards another part of the room. But this the old gentleman didn't notice, being now busily engaged in putting questions to Belmont.

The room now gradually began to fill, and presently a long-haired pianoforte player entered, and took his seat at the instrument. Then the dancing commenced, a good many couples standing up opposite each other, and at a certain signal diving at, and darting towards, others engaged in a similar amicable conflict; some standing still whilst others danced in and out a centre; the whole forming that singular spectacle called a quadrille.

To the reader who knows what nobody else in that room knew, except its owner, all this may appear rather odd, and at variance with that account of Mr. Murray's means with which I have prefaced this chapter. But odd or not, all this actually took place; though how it was paid for and by whom, I know not. But let it be remembered that Mr. Murray was not in such desperate circumstances as to be completely disabled from entertaining his friends. What such things as these cost, everybody more or less knows. Economy, even in indigence, might furnish a household with an annual party. There is no man, I believe, of such slender means but that by a daily abstinence from a meal for a twelvemonth, might at the expiration of that time furnish his friends with a dance, a fiddle, and refreshments, and comfortably sustain the expenses by the money saved. That Murray fasted to give his party, I will not say; but that he somehow or other managed to afford it is indisputable.

"You dance, don't you?" he exclaimed, darting across the room to Belmont, and interrupting a question that the old gentleman had meant three times to ask before, but had always forgotten it.

Belmont shook his head. "I have not danced for twenty years."

"Come, for once infringe this inactivity."

"You will excuse me, I am sure. I never dance."

"You play a rubber?"

"Yes."

"Ah, that's right, sir!" exclaimed the old gentleman. "There's nothing like a rubber. As to dancing, it's arrant tomfoolery; and the Turks know it, too. They make it an occupation —but we an amusement. Ever been in Turkey, sir?"

"No, never."

"Oh, never mind about the Turks now. The card-tables are ready for you below," said Murray; "and I'll go and hunt up a rubber for you. Mr. Lloyd, you know the way down; Mr. Belmont, will you follow him?"

He was moving away when Belmont detained him. "I have not," he said, "been in European society for some years. I like a rubber well enough; but I shall be infinitely more amused if you will allow me to sit here apart and look on."

"Now, do consider yourself at home," said Murray; "act just as you will. Anything—anything—command me." Then in a whisper he grasped his hand and said, "What do I not owe to you?"

Belmont smiled coldly; and pointing to a distant sofa, he exclaimed,—

"I will go and seat myself there. I shall not be observed, and moreover I shall have the gratification of observing the dancers."

Murray passed his arm through his, and led him to the spot he had indicated. There was a fawning attention, a pusillanimous civility about the man which Belmont noticed in silence. It was that behaviour which appears every instant about to throw itself on the ground to be trodden on. It was a genteel servility — a degrading meekness—a contemptible humility, expressed not by the tongue but by the manner: visible in every movement towards the object of its homage or its fear.

"Here I think you will be comfortable," he said; "but I am afraid you will not be suffered to remain long alone. All the eyes of the ladies are on you, and you don't know what Alice—that is, Miss Lloyd—said of you!"

The whole of this speech was meant for a compliment; but the whole of it was also true. The

ladies *were* looking at him, and as constantly as
politeness permitted. Miss Lloyd *had* whispered
to Murray her admiration of the appearance of
his guest, and this in terms by no means equi-
vocal.

Belmont replied with a slight bow, and Murray
went away. This eccentric, and doubtless, selfish conduct, on the part of the "handsome
man," attracted amongst the ladies a good deal
of surprise.

"Who *is* your friend, Mr. Murray?" asked
they.

"A China merchant," answered Murray.

"Oh, we cannot believe it!" said the ladies;
"he must. be some distinguished foreigner, with
a soul preyed upon by the doom of exile; or
another Manfred, the victim of a fatal passion!
Some Faust pining for his Margherita: or, who
knows? perhaps a poet meditating his verses!"

As the last idea seemed the most reasonable,
it was soon generally adopted; and so Belmont
was put down as a poet meditating his verses.

Had these inquisitive fair ones really known
what he was—had they had revealed to them the
workings of this man's soul—had exposed before
them the invisible passions that agitated his

heart, their love of romance would have been no less gratified, though their horror might have been unfeignedly real. Had they been informed that the motive of this man in thus secluding himself—in thus remaining alone in the midst of many—was to elaborate more surely in his mind the plot that was to ensnare and blast for ever the hopes and life of his most deadly foe—that foe, their host—to watch with the heart of a tiger, but with the eyes of a lamb, each movement, each action of *him* whose ruin alone could gratify that most darling passion of a wronged man's nature —revenge; their gaze might not have been less incurious, though the emotions that had agitated them perhaps, the revelation of his secret could alone have subdued!

What this man's thoughts were as he sat alone thus, I know not. His whole attention seemed absorbed in the contemplation of two objects— Murray and Miss Lloyd. The corner of the wall against which he was reclining, threw a shadow over his face. He was too remote from the dancers for them to perceive the fixedness of his gaze. Indeed, one of them appeared utterly oblivious to his presence. In the lover, the man Murray with his cowardice, his dread, was forgotten. The young girl by his side seemed to absorb his thoughts. When she left him, he followed her with eyes rendered almost brilliant with his love. He invariably greeted her return to him with a smile, and for longer than was necessary, retained the small hand which had sought his in the giddiness of the dance. His eyes were always bent upon her; but she rarely returned his gaze. She seemed looking, always looking at everything else but at him. Sometimes he would bow his head and whisper in her ear. Then would peal from her lips a merry laugh, and people would raise their eyes and look at her; perhaps murmur something to each other. She was a coquette. Every action was premeditated. The absence of her father appeared to have loosened the bonds of her restraint, and she laughed, and fanned herself, and darted her eyes here and there, and madly galloped about the room, with the wildness of a girl who, conscious of all absence of fear, gives the reins to her nature, and obeys each impulse of her disposition.

For a long while Belmont kept his eyes upon these two persons; and when the dance was concluded, and the fatigued dancers had seated themselves, or left the room for air, a quiet smile overspread his features.

"I can permit you no longer to remain alone," said Murray, advancing towards him. "Come, you must have a little chat with Alice, who seems positively dying to know you."

Belmont rose, and approached the young lady, who was seated by herself on the sofa.

"I have brought you Mr. Belmont," said Murray to her; "and now I hope you are satisfied."

Miss Lloyd blushed, and raising her eyes smiled at Belmont, who proceeded to seat himself at her side. Murray left them to hand some old lady down to the refreshment room.

"I am afraid I come self-recommended to you," said Belmont, "with a very bad character. Do you not think me very selfish?"

"Oh, Mr. Belmont!"

"However, if I have been alone, I owe much to you for having enlivened my solitude."

"To me?"

"Yes; the zest with which you pursued the last dance amused me beyond all measure. Why, Miss Lloyd, I am afraid you have quite exhausted my poor friend Murray."

"Now, Mr. Belmont—really—how am I to take this speech?"

"How do you mean?"

"I know you men look upon dancing as a very contemptible enjoyment. But contemptible as it may be, it is not fair that you should convert it into a subject for your ridicule."

"Pardon me, such an idea was very remote from me indeed. How would it be possible for me to entertain any other feeling than that of awe for an amusement so truly intellectual as dancing?"

"Thank you for your irony."

"What would you have me say?"

"Oh, never mind about dancing," she answered with a slight pout; "let us commence some topic more interesting."

"With pleasure. We will talk of Murray."

The pout increased.

"No," she said, in a hesitating manner; "not of Mr. Murray. You know he is stale to me— ah—er—that is—the truth is, I see too much of him——"

She fairly paused; but Belmont, instead of coming to the rescue, increased her embarrassment, by saying,—

" This of your husband, Miss Lloyd ? "

" Not yet, Mr. Belmont."

" Well, in a short time, at any rate."

She grew grave, and looked at Murray, who had entered the room, and who, though talking to some one else, had his eyes fixed upon her. Then glancing up at Belmont she exclaimed, with a smile,—

"Come, Mr. Belmont, I am waiting for an agreeable topic."

" What shall it be ?   Love ? "

" Oh ! "   She spread her fan before her face, and seemed silently laughing.

" No ; it shall not be love.   Shall I tell you why ? "

" Yes."

" Because love was made for men ; but women want something more."

" What ? "

" Faith."

" It is too poetical to be true.   If that is your opinion of us, dismiss it from your mind.   A woman bids you."

" But why ? "

" I don't know ; my own experience tells me to the contrary : though I can hardly explain myself."

" Then you think women do not care for faith in those they love ? "

" My opinion, I know, is fearfully heretical; but frankly, I do not think women want what you say. Poets make out that we do. But poets, as a rule, are the worst judges of the female heart. They write in rhyme, and they will sacrifice truth to secure harmony. A woman likes a handsome face : she likes a gentleman. As to faith, she does not know its meaning. If a man is devoted to her before her, what more can she want ? If that does not satisfy her, she will be always suspicious. For absent he may not think of her. How can she tell ? No; faith is a pretty word : but there's no such thing in life. Women know this, and act accordingly."

" Shall I tell you the reason of this opinion ? "

" If you please."

" Because you have never loved."

She bent her head and did not answer.

" There can be no love," he continued, " without faith : the one is the essence of the other; it is the animating spirit of a lovely embodiment. When the soul departs, the body perishes."

She maintained silence for a short time, and then looked up with a short laugh.

" Is this prose or poetry ? " she asked.

" Neither.   It is truth."

" Come, here is Mr. Murray; I know he is going to ask my permission to take me down to supper.   I like your conversation so well that I shall ask you to take me under your protection, and escort me down yourself.   Now, am I not bold ? "

" Why not Murray ? "

" I will not tell you—at any rate now.   Besides, here he is."

Murray came up to them, with his arm jutting out ready to be clasped by her hand.

" Miss Lloyd, supper is ready, and I——ah, Belmont! let me introduce you to a partner to take down !   Look, there is Mrs. Flaghearty—a nice old lady—you'll be charmed."

Belmont rose, and bowing to the young lady he was deserting, followed Murray to the other end of the room.

In many men such an act, after the request of the young lady, would have been simply rude. But Belmont, though he did not speak, quitted her with a gesture so full of respect, with an expression that conveyed in itself more than an apology, that Miss Lloyd, instead of being hurt

at his conduct, felt her admiration of this strange
being rapidly increasing. Intuitively she felt his
superiority : and perhaps she was conscious that
this silent rebuke, so curiously conveyed, was
merited. At any rate she accepted Murray's
arm, and went down-stairs with him—a little
thoughtful.

Before the party broke up, Murray said to
Belmont,—

" What's your opinion of Miss Lloyd ? "

" She is very pretty ! "

" Isn't she ? Rather inclined to be a flirt,
perhaps—that's about the only drawback."

" Not at all—not at all. You mistake her.
All women love admiration : and this love renders
them coquettish. It is not a drawback, it is
nature."

"Ah ! I suppose you know she is an heiress?"

" No ; I was not aware of it."

" A safe ten thousand on the day of her marriage, and at least fifteen more when the old man
dies."

" You are a lucky fellow, Murray ! "

"Am I not ? Ha ! ha ! Thanks for your con-
gratulations ; and thanks, my best friend, for a
great deal more ! "

He had again assumed the fawning tone habitual to him now when he touched upon this subject.

"Oh, say nothing of that; that belongs to the past. Pardon the question : you don't marry for money, do you ? "

"I — thank heaven, no ! It is love—pure, hearty love. The money is a secondary consideration. Love first, but the money not the less welcome."

"I am glad to hear it. I detest your mercenary matches."

"And so do I, with all my heart. By the way, old Lloyd has been asking after you a number of times down-stairs."

"Has he ? "

"Yes. Go down to him : I want you to become well acquainted. He may ask you to his house. He's a hospitable old fellow."

"He has already asked me."

"Indeed."

"Look ! here is his card." And Belmont drew it out of his pocket.

"I'm very glad of it. You seem a stranger here, Mr. Belmont, and of course society cannot be objectionable to you. A man of your resources will naturally soon command it. But still the interim may prove tedious. If I have accelerated its cultivation, I shall be truly delighted." He pressed Belmont's hand warmly; a sycophantic grasp, and a sycophantic voice!

" Farewell ! "

" You are going ? "

" Yes, with many thanks for your hospitable entertainment. Do not let me disturb your guests by bidding any of them adieu. I will slip out unobserved."

" Well, call upon me soon, and call often."

" I will. Apologise to Miss Lloyd and her father for my hasty departure, and assure them that I will take an early opportunity to avail myself of their invitation."

" I will. Farewell ! "

Another fawning shake of the hand, and sycophantic smile. But he would not desert his friend yet. He helped him on with his overcoat, darted to and fro to secure him his hat, pushed the servant aside, and held the door himself open for Belmont to pass through.

As Murray went up-stairs to the drawing-room, he thought to himself :

" I'll make that fellow think I'm devoted to

him. Like begets like; and if I can only get him to think I love him, he'll be sure to return me something of my affection. And that will serve me in two ways: it will ensure me his custom, and it will secure me his silence!"

To-morrow, and To-morrow, and To-morrow!

CHAPTER VIII.

THE LLOYDS.

THE heart of Belmont yearned for his child; but though he instituted the most rigid inquiries, though he solicited thé assistance of the police to procure him information, though he inserted advertisements in the papers, English and foreign, day after day passed by and there was no news. How could it be otherwise? He could give no description of his son's appearance; he knew his age, or guessed it with accuracy; but this alone would afford no clue to the discovery. True, he fondly imagined to perceive himself and Eveleen expressed in the boy's face, and drew in imagination a picture, with a pencil that was guided only by the love of a father. Even the very advertisements were useless, for he had mistaken the name, and printed "Frederick William Hamilton."

To the child, the name of his father had never been mentioned by Miss Godstone. He had heard of De Courcy; but knew not that it had been his mother's maiden name. He was called "Williams;" he held his parent's name to be "Williams;" and if ever his eye met his father's advertisement, he might have regarded the two first names as a coincidence, when coupled with the rest of the notice; but nothing more.

Four days had elapsed since the night of Murray's party, and on the evening of the fifth, Belmont resolved to call upon the Lloyds.

If internal pomp has anything to do with internal wealth, certainly the residence of the old gentleman by no means belied the announcement of Murray to Belmont that his daughter was an heiress. Mr. Lloyd occupied a large house in a square at Brompton—a freehold—and therefore sufficiently proclaiming in itself the owner's means. Who Mr. Lloyd was, Belmont had not cared to inquire. But from the conversation he had held with him in Murray's drawing-room, he gathered enough to convince him that, first of all, he had commenced life poor; secondly, that he was of humble origin; thirdly, that he was not a gentleman; fourthly, that he was so far devoted to his daughter, as to have declared to Belmont that she had his sanction to marry whoever she loved, providing the match were not downright dishonourable; and lastly, that he had known Murray three years, some business matters having first led to an acquaintance, which had terminated in his proposing to Alice Lloyd, and having been accepted by her.

Belmont was received with great cordiality of manner by Mr. Lloyd, who introduced him to an old lady seated in a high-backed chair, whom he said was his wife.

"You did not meet her at Murray's, because," said the old gentleman, slightly hesitating, "because—the truth is," he added, turning to his wife, "I don't think you and Mr. Murray get on very well together, do you?"

"Oh, I think so," said Mrs. Lloyd.

"My wife don't care for society at all, Mr. Belmont. Indeed, we have both come to that age when we look upon all that sort of thing as humbug, you know, sir. But then we've got a daughter, and it's not fair to suppose that she can view life with our eyes."

"No; it would be unreasonable."

"Generally speaking," said Mr. Lloyd, glancing at his wife, "mothers make it their business to escort their daughters out to balls and parties, and all that sort of thing, you know. But in my house, we reverse the rule ; the duty here becomes the father's."

"Mr. Lloyd," said his wife, speaking to Belmont, "does not tell you that I suffer from the very worst of healths. Alice," she added tremulously, as if about to weep, "knows this very well, and is quite content to go out under the protection of her father."

"That's true," said Mr. Lloyd, "but what would become of Alice if her father wasn't always willing to offer her his protection ? There's the rub, my dear."

"But it's your duty to look after your daughter's happiness," said Mrs. Lloyd.

"I don't know. I think I have pretty well done my duty in finding her the tin to enjoy herself with ! What do you say, Mr. Belmont ?'

"How is Mr. Belmont to know ?" said the wife, testily ; " you do ask such foolish questions!"

Mr. Lloyd threw a sour glance at vacancy, and gruffly murmured, " Humph !" Then added, "I'll have Aunt Bessy here."

" Aunt Bessy ! " exclaimed his wife.

" Yes. And put Alice under her care."

"And don't you intend going anywhere else

with your own flesh and blood?" said Mrs. Lloyd.

"No, I don't. I'm sick of it. What's society to me? Here I have to sit, in a velvet waistcoat and a stiff shirt, for four or five hours at a time, and for what? To see a heap of people throwing their legs and arms about, and giggling at each other, and fanning themselves."

"But you get your rubber, Mr. Lloyd," said his wife.

"No, I don't; not everywhere. Now I *can* get my rubber at my club every night, if I like, and without all the bother and nuisance of dressing for it. What do I do at a party? To sit and see a lot of men with oiled hair, parted down the middle, and injuring a good sight by wearing eyeglasses, floundering about here and there, tearing the girls' dresses worth twice their incomes. Bah! I'll have no more of it!"

At this moment, Alice entered the room. "Oh, how do you do, Mr. Belmont? I really didn't know you were here!" Then, as she shook hands with him, she said aside, smiling, "You were quite right to run away the other night, without bidding me good-bye. *You* know why!"

"Alice," said her mother, "no more parties for you!"

"No more parties for me? Why mamma, what do you mean?"

"You know my health won't permit me to accompany you; and your father declares he won't go out any more."

"Oh, papa, don't say that."

"Yes, I will," replied Mr. Lloyd; "but look here, Alice, I'll have Aunt Bessy down here for you. She'll go about with you, to your heart's content."

"Oh, that will be delightful," cried Alice.

"Aunt Bessy shall never enter this house for that purpose!" said Mrs. Lloyd. "Why, it's making a downright menial of her. Fancy asking a person to see you, merely to make use of her."

"But, she'll enjoy it," said Mr. Lloyd.

"Yes, I am sure she will," chimed in Alice.

"She shan't come, I declare!" cried Mrs. Lloyd, stubbornly. "She's my sister, and—the idea!" She seemed quite overcome with the thought.

"Well, don't let's discuss the thing now. Come, Mr. Belmont, I want you to see my pictures. Do you like pictures?"

"Very much indeed."

"All right. I'll show you something worth

seeing.   After that, we'll have a cup of tea, and then into my private room for a cigar, eh ?   I expect Murray here to-night.   Isn't he coming, Alice ? "

" I am sure I don't know, papa.   He was here last night."

" Well, and he'll be here again to-night."

" I hope he won't," said Mrs. Lloyd, aloud.

Alice said nothing aloud, but to herself, " And so do I."

The two gentlemen left the room; and Alice remained alone with her mother.   Just as the former was about to repeat the hope she had before expressed, and adding to it the protestation she had meditated, *i.e.*: that it was quite possible for the best of people to grow wearisome after a time, there came a loud ring at the bell, and Mrs. Lloyd, raising her head, said " There he is."

" Now, isn't it annoying !" exclaimed Alice.   " I wanted you to have Mr. Belmont all to yourself, that you might hear him talk without interruption; for he is really one of the most entertaining men I ever met.   But you can't now ; Mr. Murray will compel you to divide your attention."

At this moment the servant opened the door,

and ushered in Murray. He shook hands tenderly with Alice first, as was his wont; then
advanced towards the old lady, and did the same
thing, only with greater formality. His face
wore a pale, anxious, scared look; so much so,
indeed, that Alice cried, " Why, Mr. Murray, what
is the matter with you ?"

It is a curious fact that, though these two
persons were engaged to each other, the young
lady persisted in calling her betrothed by his
sirname. At the commencement of their engagement, Murray had ventured to address her as
Alice; but after a little, she said, " I am sure
you will consider me foolish for asking such a
question, but do you think it proper for two
engaged persons to call each other by their
Christian names—I mean, don't you think it
right that they should wait until they are married
before they do so ?"

Murray had emphatically answered *no*, and had
been at great pains to prove that this *no* was
correct. But observing his declamation to take
no visible effect on the young lady, to please her
—as he thought—he had conformed himself to
her views, and now he spoke to her as " Miss
Lloyd;" though sometimes his love would gain

the upper hand, and vent itself in an affectionate "Alice."

Upon a love so discreet the intelligent reader will form his own conclusions.

"Why, Mr. Murray, what is the matter with you?"

"Nothing—nothing. Why do you ask?" he replied.

"You are so pale, and appear to have such an agitated manner. Look at yourself in the glass."

He did so; and turning to her said, with a forced smile, "I really do not see anything peculiar in my appearance—at least, more than usual."

"Doesn't he look pale and careworn, mamma?" said Alice.

Mrs. Lloyd glanced at him and answered, "No; I see nothing unusual; it may be perhaps the gas."

Miss Lloyd was right. He *was* pale, and had a distressed and anxious look upon the face. But this he himself did not see. He was aware that in his heart there lurked emotions of a nature to produce such an expression; but he flattered himself he was an actor, and in disguising the feelings of his heart, he imagined he was not betraying them in his face. Miss Lloyd's remark gratified him. "Love," he said to himself, "has eyes to see what to every other eye is concealed;" and the smile that had been at first assumed grew real.

"Anxious or not," he said, seating himself by her side, "it is gladdening to me to know that even my most transient uneasiness can give you so much concern."

"Well, you are certainly paler than usual; and if mamma does not see it, I do. By the bye, Mr. Belmont is up-stairs with papa."

"Is he?" he exclaimed, with a slight start; then, after a pause, he said, "I am glad of it. I want to speak to him."

Mrs. Lloyd, seeing the two lovers engaged, took a book and commenced reading.

"Do you know anything of this Mr. Belmont?" asked Alice.

"No more than that he is a very nice fellow."

"There seems a mystery about him; doesn't it strike you?"

"Not in the least. On the contrary, he is wonderfully frank and plain-spoken."

"There, now; as you said that, your face wore

exactly the same anxious expression it had when you entered the room."

He gave a hollow laugh as he answered, "Why should I be anxious? On the contrary, have I not every reason to be glad? My happiness is so complete at the prospect of my soon calling you 'wife,' that if I have a serious or anxious thought, it is provoked by the unreasonable doubt that something may perhaps occur to deprive me of that joy." He laid his hand upon hers, and pressed it with emotion.

"I do believe you really love me, Mr. Murray."

"Mr. Murray still? Why not William?"

She beat the ground with her foot, but made no reply.

"Is this," he continued, "the first time that you have awakened to the conviction that I love you? Look—if your mamma were not present, I would fall upon my knees, and before you swear that you are my first, my best, my true, my only love! so much do I love you!"

She seemed amused at his earnestness, and then after a while said, "I must confess you are a most admirable lover!"

"Admirable!"

"Yes; so passionate, and yet so free from jealousy."

"As yet you have given me no cause to be jealous."

"That may be true. But, for instance, the other night—were you not jealous of Mr. Belmont?"

"Why?"

"Well, as a girl, I cannot answer you *why*; but you, as a man, ought to know."

"Because he is handsome?"

"That's one thing."

"Because he is rich?"

"I don't know about that; but, at all events, that's another."

"Because he is a gentleman?"

"Well."

"Because he made desperate love to you?"

"He didn't," said Alice, blushing.

"Because you reciprocated his attentions?"

"I didn't!" she answered, still blushing and speaking hurriedly.

"Then, why should I be jealous? He might possess every virtue, every grace under the sun; but if *you* still loved me, I would not envy him the possession of the greatest."

He spoke in the tone of a man who is confi-

dent that what he suggests as a possibility is an
actual fact. Here was faith at least! faith that
was expressed in the tremulous accents of his
voice; in the convulsive grasping of the hand
before him; in the passionate wildness of the
eyes—all speaking supreme love, adoration, and
truth!

"I hope papa won't be long," said Alice, suddenly. "Tea is ready—I'll go and tell him."
And she rose from Murray's side and went
towards the door. He followed her movements
now, as he had followed them in the party at his
house. When she left the room he clasped his
hands together, and exclaimed, "Oh, Mrs. Lloyd!
what a priceless gem have I secured in your
child!"

"There can be no happiness without love,"
answered the old lady, closing her book, and
looking at him over her spectacles. "I am glad
you are so devoted to my daughter; it augurs well
for her future."

"If adoration can secure happiness, she has
nothing to fear; it is hers."

"She deserves it, I believe," answered Mrs.
Lloyd, rather drily.

"Ay, that she does."

"But will it last? Love, you know, is a dream—or look, I will put it so : courtship is a dream, and marriage the waking. At least," she added, half - apologetically, "it is with most people."

"I am sorry to hear you repeat such cant, Mrs. Lloyd. This is the talk of people who have never loved; who are insensible to those sweet thoughts that clothe this fairest, tenderest, and perhaps most holy passion of the human heart. In a word, it is the language of those who have never seen your daughter."

This conclusion was fortunate ; for it somewhat mollified the rising irritability of the old lady, who by no means delighted in the imperious manner which Murray, somehow or other, had assumed when conversing with her. Still, a feeble anger remained, and she was about to make some caustic remark, when the door opened, and Alice, Belmont, and Mr. Lloyd, entered the room.

Murray rose, and shook hands with Mr. Lloyd, who exclaimed, " There ! didn't I say he would be here ? " When he did so with Belmont, he retained his hand a little in his, and looked at him with an expression that seemed to be comprehended, for Belmont faintly bowed his head in token of recognition of the glance.

"Mr. Belmont," said Alice, "I want to ask you if you don't think Mr. Murray looks pale and careworn to-night?. Mamma says no; but I am sure he does, and I want you to say yes, to assist my opinion."

Belmont glanced carelessly at Murray, who, with an embarrassed air, had gone to the side of the young lady, and was bending as if to speak to her. He answered, "I am sorry to be against you, but I really do not see any such signs as you speak of. Moreover, it would be paying you a poor compliment to say he did—don't you think so, Mr. Lloyd?"

"Ay," said the old gentleman, "where there's love there ought to be smiles. You know what—what Shakespeare, I think, says, 'With mirth and laughter let old wrinkles come:' and I hold that as a very solid precept. Life, Mr. Belmont," continued Mr. Lloyd, taking him by the arm, and speaking with all the solemnity of a man who enunciates for the first time a profound truth: "Life, sir, is short. It gives us little room to laugh, and therefore, say I, we are fools if we occupy that little room with tears."

"These are hardly words for your daughter's ears," exclaimed Mrs. Lloyd, leaning back in her high-backed chair, and folding her hands together with an impatient gesture. "Young people should be told that life is full of tears—not full of laughter."

"Now, I wish you wouldn't correct me before you know what I say! I never said life is full of tears, nor full of laughter either."

"Believe me, madam," said Belmont, gravely, "young people have no need to be taught that life has sorrows; they find it out for themselves, far, far too soon."

"Of course they do!" cried Mr. Lloyd. "Just imagine my sitting down and saying to my girl, 'Alice, mind you never laugh, do you hear! If I catch anything but tears in your eyes I shall be very angry!' A pretty father I should make, hey?"

Mrs. Lloyd made no answer, but kept her eyes fixed on the tea-caddy with an expression that said very plainly, "Never mind what you say, I know I'm right."

Here somebody said, "Is tea ready?" and Alice left Murray's side, and proceeded to seat herself at the tea-table. Where there is a want of unanimity in a family a guest never knows whether he is welcome or unwelcome. This was precisely Belmont's position. Frequently he felt that, after a little argument which ended always in a dead silence, and an acrimonious expression on the countenance of the opposed individual, Mrs. Lloyd would glance at him uneasily, as if regretting his presence. But he feigned not to notice this, but sought to dissipate the cloud upon her brow by entering into conversation with her on a topic remote from the cause of the concluded discussion.

All this while he noticed that Murray would frequently fall into fits of complete abstraction, forgetting to answer when he was addressed, and looking up with a hurried and bewildered stare after the second or third time of his name being re-peated. In these movements the expression of his face was one of anguish and terror, but as his head was usually bowed, this was not observed, except by Belmont, the rest imputing his conduct to love—Alice amongst the others.

At last Mr. Lloyd suggested a cigar, and the gentlemen rose from the table to repair to their host's room, consecrated to the fumes of tobacco. As they passed through the hall, Murray whispered into Belmont's ear, " I have something very particular to say to you. Can we contrive to leave this house together ? I can tell it to you as we go home."

" I am quite at your service, and will go when you like," replied Belmont.

" Don't you think Murray a lucky dog to get hold of my daughter ? " said Mr. Lloyd to Belmont, with a moist wink, after they had been seated smoking and drinking together for some half hour.

" I think he is," answered Belmont, glancing at Murray, who returned his look with a smile.

" And don't you think I'm a very wonderful fellow," continued the old gentleman, who, from the effects of companionship, had been seduced into a little more brandy than was his wont, and which even in that short time was rendering him communicative and jovial, " to have commenced life with half-a-crown, and to have ended it in leaving my daughter an heiress ? "

" Wonderful, indeed ! "

" I should like to know how many men can say that ? It's very easy to talk of, but in these times, sir, when every man is bent upon passing his neighbour, pilfering him too, so as to add from his friend's purse something more to his own store, I say to have piled upon a single half-crown my present fortune is an achievement of which I think I may very honestly boast!"

"Ay, that you may," exclaimed Murray.

"Take this house, sir," said Mr. Lloyd, looking round the room, "and consider it's my own property. Look at its size, sir, the extent of ground it covers, and ask yourself if it doesn't want a clever fellow to balance it, furniture and all, upon the little circle of a half-crown?"

"Sir," said Murray, "you should get your life written. Call it the 'Results of Industry,' and I warrant you it would excite immense attention. It would be a boon to every young man; such a happy precedent would act as a powerful stimulus to compel him into labour and success."

"And a good idea, too!" exclaimed the gratified old gentleman; "ain't it, Mr. Belmont?"

"Capital!" said Belmont.

"Egad, Murray, and you shall write it, too; you could, couldn't you?"

"I would try."

"Egad, and you shall when you're my son-in-law. We'll sit in this room together, and I'll give you all the leading heads, which, of course, you can work out."

" It will delight me beyond measure."

" When are you married, Murray, hey ? "

" This day two months, exactly."

" We are now in October—that will be in December, a freezing month for love," said Belmont.

" Ha, ha!" laughed Mr. Lloyd, "ain't he a lucky dog. When I married Mrs. Lloyd, she was not worth what she stood in—her clothes, for I bought 'em for her. Ha, ha!"

Murray, who was perhaps frightened that the conviviality of the old gentleman might lead him into disclosures not quite calculated to impress Mr. Belmont with a sense of the ancestral honours of the house to which he—Murray—was about to ally himself, changed the subject abruptly, by making some common-place remark. This led the conversation into another channel, and after a while the gentlemen rose and returned to the ladies.

Half an hour later, Belmont and Murray left the house together, the former having received at the door, from Mr. Lloyd, a hearty invitation to his house whenever he cared to call.

It was a cold night, and Belmont proposed a walk before they took a fly. Murray entered into the arrangement, and, lighting their cigars, they started off. They walked for some few minutes in silence, Belmont either not caring or wishing to disturb the reverie in which his companion seemed absorbed. At last, Murray seized his friend's arm, and exclaimed, in an agitated voice :—

"Did you notice anything peculiar in my appearance to-night?"

"In what way?"

"In the expression of my face, for instance."

"No—nothing."

"It has been a fearful struggle with me the whole evening to conceal my feelings. I was an idiot to come out—I might have betrayed myself."

"What is the cause of your emotion?"

"Can you not guess?"

"How should I?"

"Are you not yourself the cause? Did you not incite him to this? place the documents in his way, that he might murder me by degrees?"

He spoke excitedly, and his hand convulsively grasped his companion's arm.

"Pardon me," answered Belmont, coldly; "I really do not understand you."

"Not understand me? Great Heaven! did you not give Sloman those two papers which I implored you to burn, or to give me to destroy?"

"You cannot be mad, though your language would certainly induce me to form such a conclusion?"

"For Heaven's sake, do not tamper with me, Mr. Belmont. You know you have given them to Sloman; given them to him that he may annihilate me, ruin, blast me! You know it."

"Supposing I tell you that those two papers are in my pocket—what then?"

"Impossible—he produced them himself before me."

"Do you doubt me? Come, I will show you them."

They stopped beneath a gaslight, and, after feeling for a short while, Belmont drew out his pocket-book.

"Will you not believe me when I tell you that they are here?"

"Oh! search—search—and see."

With a cold, almost dreadful smile, Belmont opened the book, and ran his fingers slowly through the contents, inspecting the exterior of each paper as he touched it. Suddenly he started. "Good Heavens!" he cried, and, with trembling fingers he went once more over the papers. Pausing, he looked at Murray for a moment in silence; then, clasping his forehead, he murmured, as if in a sudden rage,—

"I have been robbed of them!"

"Robbed!" half shrieked Murray.

"They are not here—where can they be? I have not looked at them since I saw you; then I deposited them safely in this book, and I swear—ah!" His face assumed a stern expression, his brows were contracted, he grasped Murray almost fiercely by the shoulder. "I see it all!" he cried.

"Tell me—what?"

"Do you remember the morning I called on you at your office in the city?"

"Well?"

"Sloman was present when I requested an interview with you alone."

"He was."

"Perhaps he was angered at not being admitted into our conference. Perhaps curiosity urged him to the base act. At all events, he must have listened and heard all that I said."

Murray uttered an exclamation of despair, and buried his face in his hands.

"But is he capable of such a villanous act as listening to another's secret?"

"Capable? oh, he is the greatest villain upon earth!"

"Ah, how little did I suspect this. Alone in London, and anxious to make friends, I foolishly gave this man my address, and begged him to call."

"And he called?"

"Yes. Ah, I see it all too plainly now. What a fool was I not to have been more careful!"

"In what were you careless?"

"Listen. I gave this being a cordial welcome, mistaking him for an honest man. I supplied him with refreshments, and we were full of laughter and gaiety. Suddenly, he asked me—ah, the baseness of the intent!—how long it was since I had been to England. In order to answer him accurately, I was compelled to refer to the memoranda in this book."

"Well?"

"When I had answered him, I carelessly laid

the pocket-book upon the table, and something at that moment requiring my presence below, I left the room. When I returned, Sloman was still seated as I had left him, and the book was upon the table, apparently untouched."

" Apparently ? "

"Yes. I placed it in my pocket, and thought no more of the matter—thought not to look at or for these papers until to-night. Now they are gone, and now I know how they have been robbed."

" Sloman abstracted them, think you ? "

" Yes—the villain!" cried Belmont, stamping his foot, and speaking in an enraged voice. " Of course he must have known where I hid these papers. He had overheard the conversation, and was determined to possess these proofs of a secret which—ah! had I foreseen this—should have been at once burnt. He .availed himself of my absence to search the pocket-book, and, of course placed them in his pocket."

A murmur of suppressed agony escaped Murray's lips, and he shed tears.

" I'll prosecute him," continued Belmont, still in the same angry voice, " for this robbery. I'll have him locked up as a common thief!"

Murray clasped his hands together. "Do not —oh, do not!" he cried, "what would become of me when these papers are produced?"

"But how am I to regain possession of my property?"

"You cannot. But you—you are safe! *I* am the victim—in his power—to be ruined, broken-hearted."

The agony of the man was terrible to witness. A cold, hard smile writhed Belmont's lips, but it was too dark for Murray to perceive it.

"Well, as you will, Mr. Murray. I have been robbed; but to please you I will say nothing. Though if I had my own way I would indict him for the theft, and have the scoundrel severely punished. But the matter rests between you and him. It is cold, standing here. Let us walk on."

They resumed their way, and Murray seized his friend's arm with an almost clinging grasp.

"You are my friend!" he cried, "you are clever! Tell me, how am I to act in this terrible emergency?"

"When did Sloman show you these papers?"

"This morning."

"What did he say?"

"I cannot tell. I was too horror-stricken to pay attention to his words. All that I can remember is that he said he was poor—that he wanted money; that he had served me a long while, and had little remuneration for his services. That is a gross lie, for he now gets four hundred a year from me; much, much more than I can well afford."

"Why do you retain such a fellow in your office?"

"He did me a slight turn many years ago—and—and—common gratitude—ah, I keep him out of common gratitude."

"Well, he is certainly not deserving of it; for besides this trick, he told me something the other night which was so incredible that, had he not been half drunk at the time, I would have kicked him down stairs as a common and infamous liar."

"What did he say?" half gasped Murray.

"Why," answered Belmont, coolly, "that some sixteen or twenty years ago—I am not certain of the exact time—you had an innocent man transported for some trifle or other."

Murray let go his arm, and bounded several paces away from his side. Then, clenching his fist, and shaking it at the stars, he shouted—as he had shouted when Belmont had made the communication to him touching the scuttling of the ship " Water Witch,"—" A lie—an infamous lie ! Did he say this ? Ah," drawing near his companion again, and speaking in a whining voice, "you did not believe him, did you ? Oh, you could not—a thief, you know—a common, low, thief—he would say anything, Mr. Belmont, anything ! "

" Of course he would. I saw, in spite of his drunkenness, that it was a lie by the manner in which he told it me ; hatched, perhaps, for the occasion, to smooth the way to proving you a greater villain by the papers he had *then* in his pocket."

" That was it ; ay, you are keen in detecting falsehoods. Thanks, thanks for your faith in my honesty." He stopped, and stammeringly continued, " Honesty in all—all, at least, save this affair of the ship. But *that* was want, Mr. Belmont ! Want drove me to that."

" I suppose so. Well, I am not hard upon crime provoked by necessity. Necessity is a tyrant that will drive virtue to acts of the worst nature. But it is still virtue that commits them, of course. But never mind about this ; tell me what Sloman said when he produced these papers."

The frightful agitation of Murray rendered him incapable of speech for some minutes, and Belmont, that he might not appear to notice it, said, " Come, I will save you the trouble of reply, by informing you what Sloman wants. I have mixed much with men, and, from a habit of close observation, have got to pretty well penetrate into their thoughts and motives of their actions. You must understand that what I now say is, of course, mere conjecture. He knows that the possession of these papers places you wholly and absolutely in his power. You are safe as regards the law— for he will make nothing out of you by appealing to *that* tribunal. What he wants is your money, and he will leave you no peace until he gets all you have to give him. His demands have been already exorbitant, have they not ? "

Murray bowed his head.

" What ? "

" My whole fortune ! "

" He is cool ! What does your whole fortune comprise ? "

" My business."

" What is that worth ? "

"Formerly, two thousand a year; now, not more than from eight hundred to a thousand. Of this Sloman gets four, and my other clerk ninety."

"Well, let me tell you at once that you will have to yield to this man's demands, unless you like to go before the law."

Murray shuddered. "Oh, no, no!" he cried.

"Will you take my advice?"

"Anything—anything. I shall be guided by you."

"You must sell your business."

"I shall be ruined. It is my only support."

"Listen. You must sell your business, and must hand him over the entire proceeds. But not yet. Does he know you are engaged to be married?"

"Yes."

"Does he know that the young lady is an heiress?"

"No."

"Very good. You are married in two months, you say?"

"Yes."

"Go to him and promise that, at the end of

two months, you will give him the exact value of your business."

" Impossible ! "

" Listen yet. This is my proposition. The only one that will save you from transportation. For remember that this villain, if he finds that you will yield to him in nothing, will as certainly carry out his threats as that he is hump-backed."

Murray shuddered, but remained silent.

"You must advertise your business at once for sale, but secretly. Let the matter be effected in the presence of Sloman, that he may understand you are in earnest. Not a soul but you, he, and the purchaser, must know of this for some time ; I mean amongst your private friends. When the check is placed in your hands say to Sloman, ' In two months' time you shall have this, minus the amount that I shall deduct from it for my present expenses.' If he demands the money at once, deny him. Be firm in your denial. Never mind his threats. He will not care to execute them, for two months is not long to wait. Do you understand me ? "

" But—but—all this is impossible. What shall I do ? I shall be ruined."

" Not at all. You are about to marry an

heiress, are you not ? Very well ; Mr. Lloyd need not know, indeed must not know, anything of this matter until the marriage is consummated. Then you will have your wife's income to live upon. Afterwards, you can acquaint him with the matter of the sale of the business by degrees, excusing yourself by pleading what you will— want of connection, want of means—a thousand things."

" But Sloman will come upon me again after-wards, when he has spent his money, and I shall be then as badly off as before."

" In that case you must devise a certain means of removing him out of the way, or extracting his sting, so as to render him harmless."

" Can I not do so now ? "

" Yes, if you are able."

" But cannot you suggest to me a safe way ? "

" No. I see no other means of keeping him silent for the present than by what I have sug-gested. As for the future, you must let that take care of itself."

" Am I not in a terrible position ! " exclaimed Murray, convulsively clutching his fists.

" Not at all. Nothing is easier than to ensure your present safety. Your future is brightened by your betrothal; and as to your business, you will not be so great a loser by its sale. You tell me it is a poor concern."

"But it is my living."

"No, your wife is your living. And—an idea strikes me. Sloman will think he has completely exhausted you; and if once you can lead him to believe this, he will trouble you no more. Divulge not, by the faintest syllable, this proposed marriage. But I am tired, and shall take a cab. Your way is different from mine. Think well over what I have said, and communicate with me. I will be your friend, and do my best to serve you. Farewell!"

"Farewell!" The wretched man grasped Belmont by the hand, and then, perhaps to hide his tears, turned abruptly on his heel and walked away.

CHAPTER IX.

A CONFERENCE.

THE next morning, after breakfast, Belmont sat down, and calling for pen and paper, wrote the following letter :—

"MY DEAR SIR,

"If you have nothing better to do, will you come and take a friendly dinner with me, at half-past five this evening? *Sans cérémonie,* you know, for I am entirely alone. I have something to discuss with you, and therefore devoutly hope nothing will prevent your coming.

"Yours, very truly,

"HENRY BELMONT.

"The bearer shall await your reply.
"Frank Collins, Esq., Jermyn Street."

This note being despatched, he employed himself with the morning papers until the arrival of the reply. It came some half-hour after.

"MY DEAR SIR,

"I shall be charmed to accept your hospitable invitation. Meanwhile, I cannot but regret that you should have given me the least intimation concerning the motive of your invite; for my impatience to know what it is will be such as to render this day the most tedious in the calendar, until, at least, the hour you have appointed.

"Yours, faithfully,

"F. COLLINS."

This letter was written in a bold, flowing, manly hand, full of character, expressing at once vigour, energy, and determination. So at least thought Belmont, who was possessed of that singular idea, common to so many, that it is possible to determine the disposition of a man by the nature of his hand-writing; forgetting that he who writes much will, by-and-by, write small; that he who writes seldom will write with inelegance ; and that the birch in childhood and the clerk's stool in after years will equally conspire to affect the use of the pen, utterly irrespective of the character of the man that guides it.

At five o'clock that same afternoon, there was placed in Belmont's hands another letter, of which the contents were to this effect :—

"MY DEAR MR. BELMONT,

"On returning home last night, I sat up until a late hour thinking over your suggestions ; but at last came to the conclusion that it would be madness for me to adopt them. But this morning, my living curse, my incubus, the hunchback Sloman, has compelled me to alter my resolutions, and I write to you now—a ruined man ! He threatens, unless I instantly comply with his demand to hand him over the value of my business or the business itself, to communicate with the nearest magistrate, and to expose me. I remembered your advice, and foolishly dared him. He actually frothed at the mouth, and spat at me, swearing, with the most horrible blasphemies, that if I dared him again he would have me transported. But I must not, cannot, impart

to you in writing this man's menaces.   In my
present state of mind I know not who are my
friends or who my enemies.   The very walls
have ears!   Let me briefly say he has frightened
me into a compliance with his demands.   He
will not even wait the two months you proposed; and has now gone himself to insert in
the papers an announcement that this business
is for sale.   On the receipt of the purchase-
money, I am to hand the whole over to him,
reserving to myself literally nothing!   He has
sworn on his honour—his honour!—that he will
molest me no more when once the money is his.
Then he says he intends going to Paris.   I
write coolly, but my mind is a whirlpool.
Utterly ruined in means—or what is worse than
ruined, degraded into a perfect fear of this clerk,
who threatens me with the cruellest punishment
of the law, transportation, unless I yield to his
extortion—I remain, saving yourself, without a
friend in the world.   If you will not help me,
I must die!   Until my marriage—ay, and even
for some time after it—I must have money;
first to live with, and afterwards, so as not to
appear a beggar, until I can fabricate a story to
account to my wife for my poverty.   Any day

now may bring a purchaser, and with it, to *me*, starvation! What shall I do?

"Your broken-hearted friend,

"WILLIAM MURRAY.

"Burn this."

Belmont read this letter through twice. A wild exultation thrilled his heart, and he broke out into a long, low laugh. Every word in it seemed to bear its own delight; but the concluding lines seemed the most delicious.

"Any day may now bring its purchaser, and with it, to *me*, starvation!"

Was there any hidden joke in this expression? I know not; but this was the line at which he had uttered the laugh, so low, so long, so bitter, so terrible!

He looked at his watch, and seating himself at the table, seized a pen to write a reply; but his hand trembled so violently, that he was forced to rise and walk many times up and down the room before he could compose himself. Then he wrote these lines :—

"MY DEAR MURRAY,

"Your grief distresses me. Let the busi-

ness go, and let the hunchback, your friend,
go with it.   Better recommence life free from
him, than continue it with his threats to torment
you.   I enclose you a cheque for two hundred
pounds.   When you want more, I shall be
happy to advance it to you.   Send me by return
a promissory note—I need no further security.
Cheer up, and think of Miss Alice and her
sovereigns.

" Yours, in haste,
" HENRY BELMONT."

He had scarcely stamped the letter and placed
it in the hands of a waiter when Mr. Collins
was announced.

" Welcome ! " exclaimed Belmont, shaking
hands with him.   " You are punctual, and so, I
hope, will our dinner be."

" Dinner is ready, sir," said the waiter who
had introduced Collins.

" Good; then we'll go down and have at it,"
and, nodding to his guest to follow him, Belmont
descended the stairs and entered the dining-
room.

" Well, and has the day proved as tedious to
you as you anticipated ? "

"It has indeed, and I am come, eager to learn what you have to tell me."

"Patience. What wines do you drink?"

"A little sherry."

Belmont having given his orders, turned to Collins.

"Are you a drinker?"

"I can enjoy my glass, but—I am poor."

"Good. You told me that before, and now you repeat it. I love frankness, especially when it touches upon the declaration of such a social crime as poverty."

"But you don't esteem it a crime?"

"Not I, by the mass! but I do not love to see it in a man where there is a chance of his bettering it."

"But who is willingly poor who can become rich?"

"Millions!"

"How?"

"Pooh! twenty opportunities at least occur to every man to make a fortune. But of every thousand of our species one alone grasps these opportunities as they come before him. Of the rest, one half can't see them; the others avoid. But the *one* grows rich, and then people call it 'luck!' Luck! I detest this word; it is coined by the lazy to express what they cannot achieve."

"Ay, Mr. Belmont, that's all very well; but don't you know life is a see-saw—one half of us only can be up at the same time. It is easy for those who are already high to laugh at those who are low! Give me wealth and position, and I'll shout with the loudest of you, 'Arise, and equal us!'"

"Pardon me, your philosophy is wit, not sense. If life were as you say, a see-saw, fools would always be up—for the weight of men of sense would sink them."

"'Pon my soul, I believe there is a greater number of fools up than down. Genius and poverty are almost synonymous; and so are wealth and moral insignificance. If you want to see *sense* go to the garret; but if you look for *nonsense*, seek it amongst monied men—say the City."

"Ah, you are an officer, with the prejudices of a military man against commerce. However, the matter is hardly important enough to argue, though I believe I could turn the tables on you by irrefragable *proof*, if I had time. But my motive in starting this subject was to assure you that if you are willing to grasp it, I can place before you an opportunity that will make your fortune."

" You are kind indeed, even to think of me."

" Do not thank me yet; wait until you have heard my proposition. But, first of all, will you excuse me if I ask you some questions ? "

" Ask what you will."

" How old are you ? "

" Nearly twenty-seven."

" How are you connected ? "

" My father was a colonel in the —th Lancers. He was the son of a sea-captain, knighted for his bravery in an action with the Spanish, about three years before the battle of Trafalgar. On my father's side I consider myself pretty well off as regards respectability."

" Thank you. Do not consider my questions rude. I merely put them that I may the better serve you. What are you living on now ? "

" My pay."

" How much does that come to ? "

" Nearly two hundred a year."

" Humph ! Well, supposing I were to give you an opportunity of multiplying two hundred by ten, and making it two thousand, would you care to avail yourself of it ? "

" Before I can give you an answer, will you allow me to remind you of one fact ? "

" Which is——"

" That I am a gentleman."

" Thanks. There was no occasion to remind me of it. But do not fear; my proposition shall not infringe the limits of the charmed circle of honour. The whole subject is nothing more dreadful than a woman !"

" Do you mean marriage ? "

Belmont said yes, and eyed him anxiously. The young man bent his head, and appeared to think.

" Is she pretty ? " he asked, after a pause.

" Very."

" Rich ? "

" An heiress."

" Worth what ? "

" Ten thousand pounds on the day of her marriage ; fifteen thousand, at least, on her father's decease."

" Her name ? "

" Miss Alice Lloyd."

" A pretty face, a pretty fortune, and a pretty

name! So far, good. Well, I am agreeable, if——"

" If what ? "

" Why, if she is."

" That's your opportunity. Now go and secure it."

The two men burst out laughing, and Collins exclaimed, " Upon my honour! I am awfully indebted to you for this suggestion. But how am I to profit by it ? "

" I will introduce you to the family. You are good-looking, you are gentlemanly, and you are young,"—the young man bowed with mock gravity to each of these compliments—" and what is better than all, you are an officer; women like officers."

" Yes; but if I sell out ? "

" Well, you are still an officer."

Again the young man laughed, and then he exclaimed, "Do I carry with me the recommendation of priority ? "

" No ; you will have to fight for it, for I must tell you she is engaged to be married ! "

" Oh, hang it ! Then there's an end on 't ! "

" On the contrary, that makes the game more secure. For, let me inform you, she doesn't care

that for her intended.   She doesn't hate him, for
he's not worth hating.   But as for love, there's no
worm i' the bud there, let me assure you."

" But—"

" Come, finish this bottle; and but me no buts,
as you value my peace.   If you have any pluck in
you—and I'll swear you have—she's yours, before
twenty-four hours."

The young man grew thoughtful, and then
exclaimed,—

" But do you think it's exactly the right thing
to do?"

" To do what?"

" Why, in vulgar parlance, to ' cut another
man' out?"

" Listen.   This girl is young, amiable, full of
life, and pretty.   The man who is engaged to
her is middle-aged, sallow, *not*—believe me, for
I know it—*not* honourable, not a gentleman, and
in a word, not anything good.   Why she accepted
him, I am not going to say, for the obvious reason
that I cannot tell.   I do not believe—in fact, I
am sure—the match is not greatly desired by
either of the parents, and the whole of the matter
lies in this nutshell: that this girl, like most
girls, wanted a husband, and took the first that

came ; her parents being easy-going old souls, content with her choice, and studious of her happiness, suffer her to do as she likes. But the girl goes out and sees in the streets, and in private houses, better-looking men than her betrothed. She begins to think, and thinking, comes to the conclusion that she has been a little precipitate in accepting her man. She pines to be released, but nobody comes to the rescue. Is there anything questionable about releasing a girl from the thraldom in which she has been enchanted by her own folly ? Search the pages of Ariosto or Tasso, and you will find innumerable precedents to sanction the lawfulness of such a proceeding !" and he laughed.

"Your logic is excellent, and I own myself vanquished. But before anything can be done, let me first of all see this Miss Alice Lloyd."

" So you shall."

"When ? "

" To-morrow night, if you like."

" That will do capitally."

" Very well. To-morrow night, at half-past seven, meet me here. We will go together to the house, and I will introduce you."

" Bon."

"After I have placed the fruit within your reach, you must pluck it."

"Oh, certainly. Well, whether the matter prove good or bad, lucky or unlucky, I shall always remember you with gratitude—remember you as one who adopted the interests of a complete stranger, merely for the sake of serving him."

"Stop! Though I have seen enough of you to know that my esteem is far from misplaced, and therefore would gladly assist you to the utmost in my power, yet in this matter I am no less serving myself than I am you. It is right that you should know this, otherwise you might be tempted to consider me with more gratitude than I deserve."

"I am not inquisitive enough to inquire *your* motive in this subject, but implicitly trust to you."

"You shall have no reason to lament your confidence. But now pass the bottle, and let us talk of other matters. We have the night before us."

CHAPTER X.

LET us follow the movements of Murray for a short while.

The same morning on which the advertisement had appeared in the papers, notifying his business to be sold, Murray sat alone in his office, holding in his hand the letter from Belmont, with its enclosure of a draught for two hundred pounds. On the receipt of this communication, a momentary feeling of gladness had thrilled the heart of this wretched man; he imagined that this cheque was but the forerunner of as many as he liked to apply for; for he concluded that in Belmont he had found a man, who, touched with compassion for one whom a crime meditated, but not committed, had brought to the brink of ruin, was willing to alleviate the sorrows which his own detection of the evil and its subsequent, though inadvertent, disclosure had entailed.

When, however, he contemplated the bleakness of the present, and the uncertainty of the future, his heart again sunk within him, and he gave himself up to all the horrors of his present position. The recollection of his own folly—that folly which had sought in others assistance for the two crimes, *i.e. :* the conviction of the innocent Hamilton, through the agency of Sloman, and the perpetration of the crime of scuttling the " Water Witch," through the instrumentality of Johnson — aggravated his present doom, and worked his heart into curses against his own idiocy. Had he not given his bond, promising payment to the second mate, all this might have been avoided; for, as to the confession, it might have been countervailed by the charge of conspiracy. What could have urged him to this mad step ? He could not answer himself. It was perhaps a too blind confidence in Fortune, and Fortune had deceived him.

His other clerk, the old man, had been dismissed on the preceding evening, and Sloman had not yet entered the office. He had done no business for the last week, and this helped to render his pangs a little less acute. But still his livelihood was going from him : was about to be given away—and to whom? Great Heaven! To one of the most monstrous creatures that the skies ever sent upon the earth, to pollute with their presence Nature and humanity!

But then was he—Mr. Murray—any better?

He was aroused from his reverie by the entrance of a middle-aged man, who held a newspaper in his hand, and who pointed to an advertisement in one of its columns.

"Is this your advertisement, sir?"

"It is, sir."

"You are shipbrokers, I perceive, and are anxious to dispose of your business. What are your terms?"

"Eighteen hundred pounds, sir."

He would have said eighteen hundred pence, if he dared. For what was he to get of this money? But he knew Sloman would be present at the valuation of the property, and fear forced him into accuracy.

"Oh! have you your valuer here?"

"No; but I will go and fetch him."

"Very good, sir; and I will go and fetch mine, and then matters can be arranged."

Whilst they were absent, Sloman entered the office. His face wore a smooth, smiling expression; and his eyes twinkled and darted here and there, with the secret satisfaction that moved his soul.

When Murray returned, he did not regard Sloman or address him, but conversed with the man whom he had brought with him. Presently the other two entered, and in half an hour's time the matter was settled. But settled not exactly as Mr. Sloman had wished; for an inspection of the books proved that the business, instead of being worth eighteen hundred pounds, was only worth fifteen hundred.

Some opposition was accordingly raised by the hunchback, who protested vehemently against this mode of settlement; but as the figures were down in white and black, and as their results could admit of no possible doubt, he at length reluctantly expressed himself satisfied. Then a cheque was given and a receipt returned; the purchaser formally declared his intention of taking possession on the following day; and it was arranged that the name of the firm should still remain, only there was to be added to it another name; it was to read therefore thus:

" Spenser, Hamilton, Slous and Co."

Who the Co. was or were, Slous probably

alone knew; nor can I enlighten my reader on the motive of Mr. Sloman's conduct, in preferring to take fifteen hundred pounds to an annual income of four hundred, with perhaps a chance, at no remote period, aided by those two documents in his possession, of a partnership and a division of the profits.

But then Mr. Sloman was greedy; he wanted all his cake at once, and the result of this will appear hereafter.

"I will send," said Mr. Slous, "a clerk round at once, so as to preclude the necessity of your stopping here, should your business call you elsewhere." Saying which, Mr. Slous and the two valuers walked away together, arm-in-arm.

Mr. Sloman and Mr. Murray were now left alone. They remained eying each other for a short time in silence. At length Sloman held out his hand. "The money, please!"

There was a short pause; then Murray, crumpling up the cheque, hurled it with all his strength at Sloman's face, trembling with rage, and crying, "There's your money! take it, you creeping, mean-hearted scoundrel. You low, villanous thief!"

Sloman made no reply, but stooped down and

picked up the cheque, which he smoothed upon his knee and examined. Then fixing his keen, glistening eyes upon the face of Murray, white with rage, he muttered, "I'll have your life for what you have called me!"

"Have my life!" shouted the other, clenching his fist, and making a step towards Sloman. "Have my life! ha! you think I am in your power; but are not you in mine as much? Who hid the cheques and the bank-notes, the disco-very of which transported a man—eh? Who did this? What prevents me from turning Queen's evidence, against ye, you deformed villain. Kill me, kill me who will; but let me see this Jew hanged first!"

"Go and try it on! why don't you? Haven't you pluck enough to confess wanting to scuttle the good ship 'Water Witch,' so as to rob the Insurance Offices, eh? No you haven't! Ha! ha! go and try it on. Turn Queen's evidence, and see how nicely they'll treat you—go on!"

Sloman laughed, and pointed with his long fingers at Murray in a manner the most grotesque and horrible. His face was literally *blue* with rage, and alarmed by his cries, his demoniacal laugh, and that weird-pointing of the finger,

Murray turned sharply on his heel, and left his offiee—for ever.

The money given to him by Belmont, and an account of some three hundred pounds at his banker's, constituted his whole fortune. From this a tolerable sum was owing for his rent, which had fallen due that day. But two stars still shone with brightness in the black heavens of his future. Life was not utterly hopeless whilst Alice Lloyd and Belmont remained in the world!

For two days he remained in his house denying himself to everybody, striving to compose his feelings ere he should visit the Lloyds. He had written to Belmont a fawning letter of thanks for his money, calling him his hope, his life, his friend. In it he also acquainted him of the sale of his business, and assured him, when his emotions were sufficiently subdued to render him fit for conversation, he would do himself the "proud honour to call upon him" at the hotel.

On the evening of the third day, conceiving himself to be in the state his isolation had been designed to produce, he sallied forth, and took his way to Brompton. In reply to his summons, the servant informed him that Miss Lloyd was out drinking tea with a neighbour; that Mr.

Lloyd was away at his club; and that Mrs. Lloyd was asleep upon the sofa. Philosophically concluding that all perhaps was for the best, he made his way home again, and passed a restless night in dreams of Sloman, and his threat of murder. The next night he repeated his visit, and, strange to say, received the same reply. All were out save Mrs. Lloyd; she was asleep on the sofa! Slightly surprised, and greatly disappointed, but never attaching any other meaning than that of accident to this occurrence, he again went home, resolving once more to call upon the following evening.

In the morning, soon after his breakfast, he made his way to the hotel with a view of seeing Mr. Belmont. He was greeted by that gentleman as he had always been greeted: *i.e.*, with much affability and a certain gravity of demeanour.

"Well," said Belmont, "I suppose your incubus has left you at last!"

"I know not; I gave him the money, and I have not seen him for three days."

"Did he say he was going to Paris?"

"Yes."

"Then you may depend he has gone. He was a great scoundrel. Had it not been for you I most assuredly should have prosecuted him for his base robbery: for it was base in every sense of the word!"

"Ah! for the gratification of seeing that creature hanged, I would lose this arm—now!" And Murray clenched his fist, as he held out his right arm. "But," he continued, changing his voice, "how am I to thank you for your generosity? No words can speak my gratitude; my letter, believe me, did but scanty justice to my feelings!"

"I want no further thanks than your silence. I can appreciate all that you feel; and wish you to say no more about it. Have you seen the Lloyds lately?"

"No; I have called there twice, but have found them out."

"Humph! I took the liberty of introducing a young friend of mine there the other night; and I cannot express to you how charmed I was by your friends' manner of receiving him."

"A young man, do you say?"

"Yes."

A shadow overspread Murray's brow, and he glanced anxiously at Belmont.

"Pardon the question," he exclaimed, "but— but is the gentleman—good-looking——?"

" Ah, that he is!" said Belmont, in a voice of enthusiasm; "one of the handsomest fellows I have seen for a long time.   You will be delighted with him, I am sure."

" And how—how—did Alice receive him?" asked Murray, timidly.

" Aha! you are jealous!"

" Of my prospects; look at my position!"

He was pale, and spoke with a quivering lip. He seemed as if he were about to weep : tears to this man had now grown familiar.

Belmont's face assumed a grave expression. He averted his eyes from his companion's anxious stare, and murmured rather than spoke:—

" It was silly of me! I should have remembered."

" Great heaven! if your friend should prove my rival!"   He clasped his hands together, and fell backwards in his chair.

Belmont thought he was about to faint, and grasped him by the arm.

" Cheer up, man! how darkly you view everything!   He has not proved your rival yet; and if he should, is she not your betrothed?"

There came a long silence, and Murray remained motionless, his eyes fixed upon the ground, his head bowed upon his breast, and his arms hanging apparently lifeless by his side.

Belmont took out his watch and consulted it.'

"It is twelve o'clock; in half an hour's time I have an appointment. When shall I see you again?" he said.

"I do not know," answered Murray, in a hollow voice.

"I am going to the Lloyds' to-night," said Belmont; "and my young friend will be there. Come too, and you will see and judge for yourself."

Murray rose from his seat, and moved towards the door. He opened it, and then turning, extended his hand in silence. Belmont placed his in it, and Murray raised it to his lips and kissed it. As he did so, a tear fell from his eyes and rolled upon the hand of Belmont.

"Adieu!" he murmured.

"To-night you will be there?"

"Yes."

"Farewell."

The door closed, and Murray was gone. Belmont stood for a moment watching the tear that bedewed his hand.

"For every tear," he muttered, "that this

scoundrel sheds, he has made me weep ten drops of blood, and Eveleen——" he paused, and looking up, covered his face with his hands.

It was with a beating heart that Murray repaired to the residence of the Lloyds that evening. A vague, an undefinable presentiment of coming evil, haunted him. All day long had this feeling possessed his mind, and though he had endeavoured to drown it in the prospects that his hopes had conjured up of a happier future, darkly and dimly it rose superior to his will, and his face, worn with his recent anguish, grew more haggard in this new anxiety.

This time they were all at home, and, ascending the stairs with a trembling step, he was ushered by the servant into the drawing-room. His first glance was for Alice, but she was not to be seen; his next for Belmont's young friend, but he was also invisible. He shook hands with the old people, who, he noticed, expressed no pleasure at seeing him, and made no observation upon their having been out to him on the previous evenings. Then advancing to Belmont, who sat by himself on a sofa, he seated himself beside him, and asked for Miss Lloyd.

The old gentleman, with an embarrassed glance

at his wife, answered he really couldn't tell; but he fancied she was down-stairs, wasn't she?

"Miss Lloyd," said Belmont, "has been favouring us with some music; we have deserted her, and I am afraid she will think us rude."

"Is she alone?" asked Murray.

"No—I fancy," said Mrs. Lloyd, "we left Mr. Collins with her!" She knew perfectly well that such was actually the case; but *fancy* she thought qualified the dismal assertion.

"Who is Mr. Collins?" thought Murray.

"So I hear, Mr. Murray," said old Lloyd, "that you have sold your business. What did you do that for? Wasn't it paying enough?"

Murray started and turned pale. Then he glanced at Belmont with a look full of reproach. It was answered by a faint shake of the head.

"Who told you I had done so?"

"Why, the papers to be sure. Look here, man;" and rising, he fetched from a side-table a paper which he put into Murray's hands. "I haven't my spectacles on," he continued, "but you'll find it somewhere down here," and he pointed to a column with his finger.

A mortal paleness overspread Murray's features. He remembered that he had entrusted

Mr. Sloman with the insertion of this advertisement, and that he had not even read it himself. The first glance assured him of his madness, for the advertisement ended with, "Apply to Mr. William Murray, at his office or at his residence," &c.

He never thought of asking who told Mr. Lloyd that he had *sold* it : but he answered in a voice of forced desperation,—

"Yes, I have."

A significant look passed between Mr. Lloyd and his wife, and then the former glanced at Belmont. But he was looking another way.

"And what was the cause of your selling your business ? " inquired the old lady, in a hard voice.

"I really cannot enter into an explanation just at present, Mrs. Lloyd ; the truth is—— Where did you say Alice was ? "

" Miss Lloyd is down-stairs," answered the old lady, emphasising the *Miss*.

"I will go and seek her ; " and with the double motive of avoiding further questions and having an interview with his betrothed, he passed rapidly out of the room and went down-stairs. It was the custom of the Lloyds to keep a piano in their parlour, and in that apartment to listen to the music with which anyone cared to regale them.

On reaching the hall, he trod with a light step towards the parlour door, which stood some distance down, and peeped in. This is what he saw : —

On a sofa which was situated in the corner of the room, and which, by its position, discovered only the sides of those it supported, sat Miss Alice Lloyd and a young gentleman, both very close together, with the arm of the latter around the waist of the former. They were evidently in earnest conversation; far too occupied with each other to notice the intrusion. Twice whilst Murray stood regarding them, he observed the young gentleman bend down his head as if to peep at the girl's bowed face, after which he would resume his position, and they would continue to converse in the same low tones.

The first impulse of an honourable man would have been either to walk away at once, or to signify his presence by a movement of some kind or the other. But then Murray was a lover—he was more : he was an engaged man ; and as love and honour do not invariably accompany each other, save in the verses of the poet, Murray remained where he was, listening.

There was not much to hear, however, though he strained his ear to catch the faintest sound of their voices. Nevertheless, sometimes the voice of the speaker, perhaps prompted by his passion or his enthusiasm, would rise a little, and in such moments Murray heard enunciated with terrible clearness the words, "darling," "my first, best love," "mine," "for ever," and so forth.

He waited at least three minutes to hear if the lady would open her lips; but rage at last triumphing over his curiosity, he rushed suddenly into the middle of the apartment, and glaring at Alice, in a voice tremulous with passion, cried,—

"So, Miss Lloyd, this is what you—as a woman—would doubtless call fidelity! I thank you for the lesson; believe me, I am marvellously instructed."

At the first sound of his voice, Alice had raised a shriek, and the young man leaped to his feet, where he remained confronting the intruder. The reader will hardly require me to tell him that this young man was Mr. Belmont's friend, Frank Collins.

"What is your business here, sir?" exclaimed the young officer, indignant at this unceremonious interruption.

"Listen, young man, and I'll tell you; who are you, sir?"

"Let your anxiety to know tempt you to make some further inquiries to find out!" answered Collins.

"You shall give me your name, sir, here's mine," and fumbling in his back-pocket Murray produced a card which he held out.

"Believe me, I have no desire to know your name; simply, what is your business?"

Murray looked as if he would have knocked him down; but stifling his rage, he turned to Alice and cried, "You know who I am—you—tell him! have you forgotten me?—tell him!"

"If you please," interrupted Collins, "do not forget that you are addressing a lady."

"Is it thus," continued Murray, not heeding the interruption, "that you repay me for my devotion? is it thus that you requite me for a love which, as the inspirer, you should at least pity and respect!"

He spoke in a manner that, had not the expression of his face fully disclosed the fact, could have left no doubt of his sincerity. He moved towards the door slowly, as if expecting to be recalled, but she spoke not. Once more he turned towards her. "Am I to conclude that you have cast me off for ever? I, for whom you have professed an honest attachment,—am I to believe that a stripling has supplanted me in your affections, ejecting me from that hold upon your heart which you led me to believe—which my own heart whispered—I had?"

Either annoyance at being detected with Mr. Collins; rage at the abrupt entrance and angry demeanour of Murray; or disgust at his pale, haggard, careworn appearance, his blood-shot eyes, his disordered hair, his *tout-ensemble* that spoke the very essence of wretchedness; held Alice dumb. Contrasted as he was with the fresh, youthful, handsome appearance of the young officer, surely he presented a most piteous spectacle. He stood hovering in the doorway for a few moments, casting really heart-broken glances at his late love; but finding her mute, he suddenly cursed her with a terrible blasphemy, unmeet for my reader's eye, and rushed from the room. Grasping his hat, which lay upon the marble-slab, he jerked open the hall door, and without casting a glance behind, fled into the darkness beyond.

He walked on with a wild, irregular tread, looking neither to the right nor left, but with his eyes fixed on the ground, and muttering incoherently to himself. He was aimless, hopeless. He went whither the streets led him, and one after the other he passed, unconscious where he was, still muttering to himself, still with the wild, irregular tread.

Suddenly he came opposite a large butcher's shop, with its rude gas-streams flaring into the air; the ruddy light seemed to annoy him, for he drew his hat over his brows and crossed the road. Onward still, down this alley, up this street, still pressing on, unwitting of his destination, only— that he was hopelessly ruined. Men eyed him as he passed, and whispered to each other, thinking him mad.

At last he came to a bridge, and here he paused. Yet he knew not why he paused. There was a toll-gate through which he had to pass, and the keeper had shouted to him for money. Mechanically he had felt in his pockets. and flung down some half-pence. There was a penny too much, and the keeper had offered it

him back, but he had passed on, and was some
distance away. In the centre of this bridge he
paused, and looked over into the trickling current
below. Most inviting it was—cold, and desolate,
and dark. But cold as it was, to his heated,
throbbing brain it was boiling; desolate as it
appeared, compared to his heart it was joyous
and smiling; dark as it looked, compared to his
present, it was brilliant with a thousand whispered promises.

What is there in this river that exercises over
the broken-hearted such a frightful fascination?
There seems to be no repose within it! it is
always eddying in little whirlpools against the
buttresses of the bridge, or upon the slimy sides
that are mirrored in its margin!

With his head supported in his hands, and his
elbows propped against the low stone wall, he
stood leaning thus and looking over, like the
ghost of some segment of our vast human circle,
gazing at its own corpse that washes to and fro
beneath it. Suddenly a heavy hand was laid
upon his shoulder, and glancing up with a cry,
he perceived Belmont standing by his side.

" Is it suicide ? "

" Go—go ! " Murray said with a shudder; " go

—you have brought me to this. I was at peace with the world and myself before I saw you—now look on me!"

"What is there to be seen?"

"Seen!" he shouted fiercely, turning and confronting his companion; "seen; do you ask? I will tell you! The shadow of one who had hopes before him which your presence blasted! who had happiness near him which your presence blighted! who had love for him, and within him, which your presence crushed? Seen! do you ask? Oh, mockery, mockery! better that I had been sleeping years ago beneath the waters of that black river, than that my eyes should have been opened to see such as *you!*—such as *you!* —and to bring me to this!"

"You are mad. Come home with me; to-morrow you will wake in your senses."

"Mad;" he muttered, turning his face again to the river, and resuming his old position; "it would be well—very well for me—if I were mad! What brings you here?" he added with a cry, but without looking at Belmont. "Your presence has blasted my life—why still haunt me?"

"I followed you from the Lloyds' fearing that

you might have been tempted to commit some rash act. You did not see me, but I was behind you the whole way, watching you for some moments as you stood, just as you are standing now. Then I addressed you."

"Why? What do you want of me?"

"You are a ruined man——."

"I know it!" Murray shrieked, leaping from his place and throwing his hands up; "why tell me what I know."

"You have lost the darling of your heart—the girl you lived for, would have endured all for—gone!" Belmont said, in a voice softened by the sympathy it seemed intended to convey. "You are alone—the world a desert to you—your present, dark—your future, desolate!"

"Go on!" Murray hoarsely exclaimed, clutching Belmont's arm, and looking up into his face, with the expression of a man whose brain is crazed with woe; "you are well schooled in the names of my complaints—they run smoothly upon your tongue! Proceed! recapitulate! I love to hear you talk thus—*you,* the cause of the miseries it seems so sweet for you to rehearse!"

But Belmont continued with an imperceptible

smile, but in the same quiet voice, "You are right in upbraiding me; I confess myself to have been the cause of your present lot. But see how wilful Fate is in forcing me into acts to the results of which she took such heed to blind me! You think me your enemy; but did I act as one when, after communicating to you my discovery of your crime, I swore to you not to betray it? Did I act as one when, amidst your anguish, I endeavoured to comfort you with sympathy and advice? Did I act as one when, with certain poverty staring you in the face, I provided you with means to leave you comfortable—ay, and offered you more, that you might prosecute with success a scheme of love of which had the conelusion been favourable, happiness and affluence would have been yours! Remember I was a stranger to you—what claims had you upon me for all this?"

He paused and keenly scrutinised the features of Murray, which were upturned and partially visible in the night light from the sky. But the man remained silent, and Belmont continued: "A scoundrel, who was your foe, robbed me of what I had sworn to you not to disclose. Was that my fault?"

Murray clenched his hand and shook it, but made no reply.

" If *he* has brought you to this, do not upbraid me for it. Was it possible for me, an unsuspicious man, to contend against the basest kind of thief, and the foulest kind of spy ? "

" But Alice—Alice ! you severed my Alice from me ! She was my all to me. I loved her, sir ! oh ! I loved her well. I reposed my hopes on her —the very life-blood of this heart," smiting himself upon his breast, " owed its circulation to this love. It was adoration, sir—oh, it was worship. Perhaps you have never loved ! Then you cannot pity me. But 'twas cruel—cruel to rob me of my love—it was cruel—cruel—cruel ! "

His voice faded to a whisper, but his lips continued mutteringly to repeat the word " cruel," his hand the while smiting upon his breast, and his eyes fixed and staring at the sky.

At the words " perhaps you have never loved," a hard smile had gathered round the mouth of Belmont, which, contrasting with the frown upon his brow, gave his face a startling and singular expression. He laid his hand almost violently upon the shoulder of Murray, and said, " Were it not too late, you might have had your rival——"

"What?"

"Transported for an invented crime."

Murray gave a sudden start, and fixed his eyes upon Belmont.

"Who told you this?"

"Told me what?"

"There is a meaning in your words—I know—know—ah! it was Sloman!"

"Your language is incoherent; pray be calm and compose yourself!"

"Ay, it was he—he revealed himself! Oh, but he was a scoundrel, sir. If he told you this, never believe him. A thief, a spy, you know—never believe him, Mr. Belmont—sir—dear sir—a liar, an arrant, impudent liar!" He was certainly growing mad. His hands were shaking like an aged man's, and it appeared as if he were rather rehearsing to himself the excuse he intended to speak, than actually addressing his companion.

"Come," said Belmont, "let us leave this cold place. I have a proposition to make to you. Before long, I intend going to Paris. If you like, you shall accompany me. This Sloman is there; and since you have no hope left, create one by making revenge a hope. Revenge yourself!

Sloman, not I, has brought you to this; he has your money: he has your secret. Follow me; and if an opportunity presents itself, you shall grasp it for the love of vengeance."

"I will!" Murray cried, his eyes flashing, and his clenched fist raised above his head; "I will accompany you! We will seek the Jew together; Ay, hunt him down! It is a noble thought. *He* has brought me to this—you are right. We will go; I will dog him through every city in the world, though my feet bleed with the walking. What have I to fear! Death? Death is the only thing that is left for me now in this world—after this revenge. Ah, 'tis a noble thought. Come, good sir, come, I am impatient to start. When do you go?"

"You shall come with me to my hotel; there we will talk the matter over."

Murray seized his arm. "I was wrong to upbraid you," he said, with the tears trickling down his face; "you are my good friend, after all. Ay, and we'll both have at this deformed imp together — we are strong together, sir — you for the theft; I for—" He paused, then looking around him shrinkingly, he muttered, "Come, it is cold; very cold. The river smells.

Pah ! how black, how muddily it flows. Come—
there is hope yet—hope whilst Sloman lives—
come ! ”

And with a shudder, Murray walked rapidly
away by the side of Belmont.

.

END OF VOL. II.

BRADBURY, EVANS, AND CO., PRINTERS, WHITEFRIARS.

Lightning Source UK Ltd.
Milton Keynes UK
UKHW011525090119
334994UK00008B/890/P